LATENT
DAMAGE

London detectives hunt a vigilante killer

IAN ROBINSON

Published by The Book Folks

London, 2021

© Ian Robinson

ISBN 978-1-913516-79-6

www.thebookfolks.com

Latent Damage is the first novel in the DI Pippa Nash and DS Nick Moretti mystery series. Details about the other books can be found at the back.

PROLOGUE

Jared Hussein's life was about to end. He took a glance at the cards he'd been cradling for the last five minutes. A fanned selection he hoped would bring him success after a day's accounting for the North London mosque where he was the trustee and figures man. The accounts were in order and healthy, which is more than he could say for his current hand.

'I'm out,' he announced as he lay down his cards and waited for the victor to show theirs. It had been a good night despite his loss, and he felt no resentment at handing over the monies owed.

He collected his coat, putting it on over his thawb and added a woollen beanie in preparation for his exit from the terraced house where he'd been enjoying the company of friends. He bid the three remaining players goodnight as he climbed the basement stairs to the house's main door. He patted his coat pocket and reassured himself he had his house keys. He didn't want to wake his wife and child. Satisfied he had everything he'd come with, aside from three hundred pounds cash, he exited the house. The December air greeted him like a cool slap as he ducked into his coat and made towards his own abode. His place was three doors down from the mosque. As he walked, he checked his watch and decided he needed to pray.

He enjoyed the mosque, the camaraderie, his faith, and Allah. All meant the world to him. He knew his gambling wasn't in accordance with his beliefs and was sure to not use any monies gained by this activity as Zakat. This assuaged his troubled mind as did the prayer he now absorbed himself in. On completion of the words, he left

1

the mosque after embracing the imam and whispering he would see him later. The imam smiled warmly saying, 'Inshallah.'

Hussein stepped out the door and turned right and, as he got to the front of the mosque, the bracing night air rushed through his thawb and reminded him he'd forgotten his coat. He turned to walk back and as he did, he looked up to the minaret.

He heard muffled footsteps but was too slow to turn. His body jolted as his forehead was grabbed from behind by a gloved hand and jerked back to expose his throat. A knee dug into his thigh and held him against the railings of the mosque. He froze as he felt the pressure of a sharp edge against his throat in contrast with the warm breath of his assailant that flicked across a tiny bald patch at the top of his skull as though his hunter was scenting its prey.

His arms were incapacitated in a single-armed bear hug. Robbed of speech through fear, he let out a final sigh as the surgically sharp blade was drawn with purpose across his neck, severing his jugular. The legs that had supported him for fifty years collapsed as he crashed to the pavement. As he lay there he felt a gloved hand pat his chest and, as his vision blurred, he saw a pair of trainers as they reflected in a pool of blood before they disappeared from sight.

CHAPTER ONE

Moretti knew the moment he placed the phone back in its charging cradle that his holiday was hanging in the balance. It came with the territory, when the team you worked on are "in the frame" for a new murder two weeks before you are due to go away for an all-inclusive break in Corfu. It was the last call Detective Sergeant Nick Moretti wanted to receive. The team had a number of cases on the go as it had been a busy year for murder but so did every other murder team in the Met's Homicide and Serious Crime Command.

His bedside clock glowed 05:00. His work mobile phone remained where he'd left it, out of charge, on his bedside table. Thankfully, his immediate superior, Pip Nash, had the foresight to carry the home contact numbers for her on-call detective sergeants.

Moretti had previous for not keeping his mobile regularly charged and on. It wasn't a case of being work-shy; keeping a gadget alive all the time was just not the type of detail that occupied his mind as much as it did hers.

Moretti eased his legs out of bed, stretching out his muscles to reactivate them for an extended period of work. He got up and plugged in the mobile to get some juice in the battery while he took a shower and got dressed in a dark grey suit with a plain tie, white shirt, and black brogues.

He'd owned the boat since 2010. The landline he had to have on insistence of Nash. As much out of accessibility for her as for his welfare and safety.

He found his work keys where he always left them in a carved wooden bowl in the shape of a grenade. The words "For Shrapnel" burnt into the wood. He picked up the grab bag he carried with him when he was on call, which contained everything he'd need to attend a crime scene without having to go back to his base at Hendon Training School.

On his way to the car park, his gaze fell upon a woman walking along the jetty carrying a pair of heels, a pair of Converse trainers now on her feet. She blew smoke rings into the air as she strode, her right hand pointing the cigarette to the sky, her blonde bob and the roll of her hips accentuated by her movements. Moretti hitched the bag farther up his shoulder as he got nearer to her.

'Morning, stranger,' she said, with a joyous lilt in her voice.

'Morning,' Moretti acknowledged in a tone that was courteous and unreserved.

They passed each other with a high five, both turning to walk backwards along their own routes as they continued speaking.

'Rough night?' Moretti asked.

'All hands no cash,' she replied with a playful roll of her blue eyes as she raised her eyebrows.

'You?' she asked.

'Just leaving. Catch you later, maybe?'

'Sure, just knock. I should be about, I've no plans,' she said as she turned and headed towards her own narrow boat moored four down from his. He watched as she turned. A part of him wished he was going back to bed and not to work. The investigation of death was a priority though and duty called as Nash was already on scene, and had been the moment the job broke.

CHAPTER TWO

The traffic was busy for such an early Saturday morning in December.

He approached the junction opposite Finsbury Park underground and took a wide swing just as another officer stepped out of the road and onto the pavement. Moretti brought the car to a sudden halt and terminated the blues and twos.

Throwing the vehicle's green plastic logbook into the crevice between the dashboard and windscreen, he checked to ensure it displayed the Met Police writing. The logbook now became a sign for all cops and traffic wardens that it was a police vehicle and not to be touched or removed on pain of death. A small number of onlookers had congregated at the crime scene tape marking the outer cordon. The majority in traditional Islamic dress, all craning their necks to try to catch a glimpse of what lay beyond the barrier. They remained calm and pensive. A few members of the press had gathered and, to Moretti's right, a tired-looking reporter gave a commentary to the camera. Moretti pressed a button on his key fob and popped the boot of his car open.

News must be scarce, he thought as he sat on the boot's opening and began to empty his mind of the journey and all the frustrations of London traffic to focus on the job he had ahead.

The call that morning from DI Nash had informed him that she had been called out by the Homicide Assessment Team and was at the scene of a suspicious death and his presence was required. Detective Inspector Pip Nash was the Senior Investigating Officer and it was her job to make the judgement call to get her DS woken up and have him attend to assist her. He didn't mind that because it was his job to respond when she called. They'd worked together as detective constables on a Borough crime squad ten years ago. She headhunted him to her Murder Investigation Team on hearing of his recent promotion. At first, he'd refused as he'd worried it might affect their friendship. She'd assured him it wouldn't and that she needed his skill and sound judgement more than she needed a beer with a mate every now and then.

As he pulled on his forensic suit and looked for his shoe covers, a young PC approached him and handed over an outer cordon log.

'Busy one?' Moretti enquired of the officer as he doubled up his latex gloves. He noted the constable looking at the warrant card attached to a blue lanyard around his neck.

'I should have been in custody tonight, gaoler duty, so I'm not complaining,' he responded.

'You should value that role. Main source of contact with your local villains and a great way to get to know faces and recruit informants,' Moretti said as he scrawled his name, rank, and time of entry on the sheet and handed it back to the officer who nodded his thanks.

He shut the boot and ducked under the tape the officer had lifted for him just as a reporter finished her take, having become aware of his arrival. The reporter didn't know him personally, just that any plain-clothes officer who turned up and donned a forensic suit meant something serious was going on.

'Excuse me? Sandra Wilcox, BBC News. Is there any truth that this killing is a right-wing attack against the Muslim community?' she asked, waving her microphone like a wand as she approached him.

She'd need more charm and a better spell to make him talk. Moretti blanked her and carried on walking towards St Thomas's Road and the crime scene tent that had been erected on the path outside the North London Central Mosque.

Scenes of Crime Officers were busy photographing the area and a white flare of light burst from inside the tent as he approached the inner cordon. The fact it hid what was beneath its canopy was secondary. Victims deserved justice as well as having their dignity maintained. At the inner cordon, a PC approached him carrying a clipboard and pen and asked him to sign in.

The tent flap opened, and a figure exited. She was dressed head to toe in her crime scene suit; he knew who it was as she carried a clipboard with "hands off" written in Tippex on the back and no one would dare touch her board. DI Nash approached him as she pulled down her facemask hiding her nose and mouth.

'This one's got political fallout written all over it,' she said as she looked back at the tent.

Moretti raised his eyebrows. Politics was of no interest to him but he knew she was always keen to avoid it. Like Nash he was concerned with ensuring as much evidence as possible was captured during the golden hour and the further twenty-three. He'd leave the political debate to her and those higher up the food chain.

'What have we got?' he asked as they approached the tent's entrance.

'Victim's had his throat cut. You'd better take a look,' she said. Moretti noticed her eyes looked red as first light began to break over the minaret. The weak sun's strength cast a shadow over the tent and provided a spiritual calm over the sombre scene. Nash nodded at Moretti and they entered.

Next to the victim there was a Scenes of Crime Officer shining a torch over a large gaping wound in the victim's throat and the significant pool of blood that had formed under him and found its way into the cement joints of the path. Another SOCO was making notes and dealing with the evidence bags and exhibits. Alongside him was another figure with their back turned away from the entrance to the tent.

The victim was face down having dropped forward into railings then slumped to the pavement. The front of his face was obscured but still intact. He wore an ankle-length white cotton thawb and on first appearance was no older than fifty.

His arms were splayed wide and Nash surmised he must have hit the railings with a shock and force that didn't allow for stopping the assailant with his hands. His left-hand ring finger displayed a wedding band and on his wrist was a watch. A family man, she thought and bent down and looked closer. The watch was a Rolex and appeared to be genuine.

Moretti looked up from his crouched position.

'How many times was he slashed?' he asked the person next to him.

'Slashed? Who's saying he was slashed?' The voice of the pathologist, Dr King, penetrated Moretti's ears as he looked up from the body of Mr Hussein.

'Sorry, Doc, I didn't know it was you,' Moretti said as King got up and stood alongside the SOCO.

'Glad you decided to join us, Sergeant – just as we're nearly done. Remarkable time-keeping as I've come to expect from you.'

All eyes were now cast down at the view before them as Dr King continued, 'From what I can see of the injury, which is very restricted due to his position at the moment, it looks like a very clean cut. It's as though he's been in surgery and left hospital after the first incision. I'll know more later when I can examine the poor fellow in better light and conditions back at the mortuary.' Dr King turned to Nash, she smiled in appreciation at his attendance and he left the tent.

A breeze hit the side of the tent and the unexpected movement startled the living occupants.

'Let me know once he's moved. I don't think we're looking at a robbery,' Nash said to Moretti.

He nodded his understanding.

Nash leaned in towards Moretti's right ear. Better to converse inside the tent than out. Reporters had a canny way of reading lips or even filming a conversation and having a professional lip-reader look at it after. The early interest in the crime bothered her, and the impact on the community was going to be significant.

'Get the house-to-house organised. I need all CCTV seized from wherever we can find a camera within the immediate vicinity and surrounding streets. I'm particularly interested in those that overlook the front of the mosque. They must have cameras in there too. Get a specialist search team down here to look for the weapon. You never know, the killer may have discarded it,' Nash said to Moretti.

She placed her hand on her chin and looked down at the body. By the victim's side was a clear exhibit bag and within it was a single playing card of the ace of spades that had been removed from a small pocket on his thawb. The lifeless form in front of her was a husband, friend, and son to someone. Someone she'd need to trace quickly before the news got out.

But, from the shouting and screaming coming from outside the tent, she realised it had already got around. Moretti was the first to leave, and she followed.

The noise was coming from the Seven Sisters Road. A loud, guttural, raw sound. A sound she knew from experience: the sound of grief. A woman dressed in a niqab was near the tape and a man, dressed similarly to the deceased, was stood near her but not offering any physical contact.

Her legs were unable to support her sorrow and angst and her body gave way as she gently lowered herself to the floor. A uniformed officer approached and placed a silver foil blanket around her shoulders. He looked up and saw Nash approaching and the young officer indicated she should follow him away.

'I'll get on with the other arrangements,' Moretti said as he moved back towards the main scene.

Nash walked over to where the PC was standing a good distance away from the small crowd. The reporter couldn't be seen, much to Nash's relief.

'Sorry to get you away, ma'am, but I didn't want you going over there until I'd spoken to you.' The PC sounded sincere and Nash was glad she had a copper with common sense on the cordon. She knew how vital the role was to keep people out and let the right people in.

'Go on,' Nash requested keeping her facemask up.

'The lady on the floor is claiming her husband's the man in the tent. She says he never returned home last night, and that's unusual for him. The man with her is the imam from the mosque. He's told her he'll speak to you for her. I've told her that until a formal identification is made, we can't be certain who it is. She's having none of it though. Oh… and the Borough Commander's on his way down, ma'am. Thought you'd want a heads-up on that.'

'Does he not need sleep? Thanks for that…?'

'Jack, PC Jack Adams, ma'am.'

'Thanks, Jack. Your next job's preventing the Commander passing through. No matter what he says, he cannot go beyond your scene tape. I'll see him when I'm done. Is that clear?'

'Crystal.'

With the exchange complete, PC Adams signed Nash out and turned to face the road to await the unwanted arrival at his cordon. Nash headed towards the imam. She approached slowly, removing the forensic hood from her head and dropping the mask around her neck.

'*As-salam o alaykum.* I'm Detective Inspector Nash. Do you need medical aid?' She crouched to the level of the woman directing the question at her and not the imam whose eagerness to be included in the conversation was obvious.

'*Wa alaykum as-salam.* All I need is for my husband to come home and I know that won't happen,' she said as tears fell from her large brown eyes.

Nash let her take a few breaths in the hope that she'd explain more but she didn't. Her eyes settled on the imam who continued where she'd left off.

'Detective Inspector, it was I who told her. It was impossible for me not to as I found him. I called an ambulance as I thought he'd had a heart attack, but it was only on getting to him that I saw… well, you know what I have seen.' He stopped and hung his head, moving his prayer beads through his fingers, his actions making the woman open up to her grief.

Nash could see little would be achieved at this point. She nodded at the imam and phoned Moretti. He answered on the second ring.

'I'm going to need a Family Liaison Officer down here. Whoever you send, tell them to meet you first so you can speak to them. I can't explain anything further on the phone.' She hung up once he'd confirmed her request.

'I'd like you both to wait here with the officer,' she said, pointing to PC Adams.

'There'll be a plain-clothes officer along shortly. They'll need to speak with you both and take statements. I appreciate what you've told me, sir,' she said and the imam nodded.

As Nash finished with the imam, she glanced up to see the figure of a man in full dress uniform approaching. From the insignia on his shoulder, Nash knew the Commander had arrived.

Another officer, or bag carrier, as they were known, scuttled alongside him trying to match his lengthy stride. PC Adams had seen the same and began rocking from heel to toe in anticipation of the Commander's arrival.

'Morning, Jack. Where's DI Nash?' the Commander asked as he looked over the crime scene tape hoping to get a visual of the scene that had been causing him headaches since the barrage of calls from various community representatives. Many had demanded to know why access to the mosque was sealed off and preventing prayer. The last one being Maghrib – the last time Jared Hussein got to convene with his God.

Nash could put it off no longer. She nodded at the imam – shaking hands with a woman was not something he may have approved of – and excused herself as she walked towards the Commander.

'DI Nash?' the Commander asked.

'Yes. How can I help you, Commander?' Nash responded in a tone that expressed he should get to the point as she had a job to do and little time to waste.

11

'How much longer until you release the scene? I've taken numerous calls, and we need the mosque back in use immediately.'

'Well, crime, like murder, gets measured in lengths of string, sir, and right now the ball's unfurling,' Nash replied bluntly.

PC Adams stifled a laugh at her rebuff.

'I understand you have an investigation to manage, Inspector, but I have the community to deal with. These situations have a tendency to get hostile when it comes to religious practice being prevented by tents and tape. You must have a ballpark timeframe I can feedback?' the Commander asked.

Nash looked away, squinting into the rising sun and accepting the early morning breeze with comfort, safe in the knowledge she was fortunate to experience it unlike the poor sod on the ground.

'It will be removed when I'm satisfied it's no longer required. There's nothing more to be debated, sir. I'm certain you can appreciate that when you look at it from an investigative angle and not a community one.' Nash began walking towards her car.

'Detective Inspector, I haven't finished.' The Commander's voice raised enough to cause people to turn in his direction.

'With respect, I have. I'm needed elsewhere and will make sure you're informed as soon as the mosque can be re-opened. Unfortunately, the victim fell where he did. He was given no choice and, by default, neither have I.' Nash got back to her car and after removing her suit, she placed it in a bag for incineration and taped it up.

As she got into the driver's seat, she could see the Commander had found the imam. Nash started up the engine and reversed. Her next destination was Hendon. She'd seen what she needed to and was happy to leave it in Moretti's capable hands.

CHAPTER THREE

The newly built office building at Hendon Training School accommodated Nash's team. It was alive with the low hum of voices and the clinking of spoons on china as detectives grabbed a well-earned brew. Her squad now re-assembled from all parts of London and the Home Counties where they lived, or had spent the night, as was the case with some of the single members of her team. Nash always felt proud of her unit when a murder broke. She could rely on each one to respond when the balloon went up requesting all hands on deck for a new job. She entered her own office and dumped her bag. A fresh coffee steamed as she took a welcome sip. She opened the top drawer of her desk pod and removed another sugar sachet: it was going to be a long day, week, or worst case, month and the extra sugar was needed.

A couple of detectives were already out conducting house-to-house and the FLO was in attendance as she'd requested. She would need to brief her inside team: the people that ran the hub of any murder investigation.

Prior to computerisation, any major enquiry had been collated using index cards. The computer brought the arcane into the digital age and the detectives could now access the main system via an app. Some still found the adjustment a challenge, one of them being her office manager, George – a former career DC who'd reached his thirty years' service and had returned as a civilian to his old role.

Her office window sported a race between droplets of rain as a contingent of new recruits practised drill for a future passing out parade. Some marched like an octopus, arms everywhere but straight, others ambled as though it was a Sunday stroll. As she drank, she wondered which one of them would be destined for detective duty and enter her world of murder and mayhem. She also pondered how many would last a year out on the streets.

She'd already been given notice that a number of detectives who'd enlisted as direct entrants would join the Homicide Command at some point, a thought she pushed aside as she wished to remain focussed and didn't want to dwell on situations out of her control. Nash's team had earned the right to be on the command. She'd embraced the detective career path herself and there was nothing she wouldn't do that she didn't expect her team to do too.

She turned back to her desk as her landline summoned her attention via a low tone and flashing light on line one.

'Nash, MIT 2.'

'Ma'am, we're done here for now and on our way back. The victim's on his way to the mortuary and PC Adams agreed to travel with the body for continuity. I think he'd like to join Homicide after what he's seen. Anyway, the victim's wife is coming to the mortuary for the identification so that will be taken care of. SOCO are conducting some final tests, for what I didn't ask as they were too occupied in their jobs. Dr King has called and stated the post mortem is at 4 p.m. today.'

'Great work, Nick. See you when you get here.' Nash ended the call and took herself and her coffee through to the Intel cell.

* * *

The squad assembled in the briefing room and Nash did a quick head count before she sat down and began. Each officer had come prepared with a notepad and pen ready to receive instructions.

Despite computerisation, Nash still preferred an old school approach. She utilised a board displaying a timeline and images of those involved in the investigation. As the enquiry progressed, the board would fill up with associative links: names, addresses for work and home, phone numbers, vehicle index plates, and places frequented. At present, the board displayed the name of the victim as the team awaited an image from the family appropriate to be displayed and viewed. She didn't use the scene photos of victims unless it was warranted. She wanted her team to stay aware they were once alive and loved, not a bloodied heap on a London pavement.

If the computer systems failed, she had the board as a backup. Plus, when the officers returned to the office, they could see any progress immediately. At night and when outsiders visited, the board would be covered by a sheet. The information wasn't for everyone's eyes.

Nash began the briefing. 'I appreciate we don't have much to go on at present. I'd like a run-through from those at the scene, so we all have the same knowledge of where the investigation's at. Let's start with house-to-house.' Nash looked up at DCs Reardon and Faulkes who'd been on that duty.

DC Reardon, the elected speaker of the two, began.

'Well, we covered those who'd been in the mosque first as they'd been kept back by uniform. Nothing forthcoming as they were all inside at prayer. Surrounding houses were all the same. Nothing seen or heard. We're back later as some occupants never replied and could've been asleep or out,' he said.

'Thanks. What about CCTV opportunities? Where are we with that?' Nash asked and DC Squires responded.

'Too early to say, guv. I'm back at the mosque again later today. The surrounding area has some cameras, and enquiries are in hand with the council. From what we have managed to find and view, the victim's route is corroborated with the family's explanation of his movements.'

'Very well. Initial cause of death is a single cut to the jugular. I will update you after the PM of any other developments. Get your actions from George and let's start getting some background on the victim's associates. We're still establishing where the assailant was prior to the murder but we're hopeful this will be ascertained soon. Any other business?'

'Just one thing,' Moretti said as he entered the room. 'The biscuits are disappearing at a phenomenal rate, so try to be reasonable with the amount you take, or the tea club money will go up.'

'You listening, George?' DC Reardon commented.

'Not guilty. I have my own, as those on the inside team know.'

'Your own? Why's that?' Reardon asked.

'Because I never know where your hands have been, that's why,' George replied with a smile.

'Well, getting your hands dirty is what being a detective is all about, Georgey boy, or have you been inside too long to remember that?' Reardon said with a smirk.

George gave him the middle finger. All of it in good humour and taken as such by those around the table.

'Just be mindful about how many we *all* consume and please clear up after you too as the mess is out of order for the cleaners to deal with,' Moretti said.

'One last thing,' Nash said as the officers began getting up to leave. A few groans could be heard from the group. 'Your work this year has been tremendous. It's been a busy year and I appreciate we're all exhausted and could do without a fresh job. If any of you need anything or some time off, then come to me. I can't guarantee you'll get it as we have a new enquiry with no suspect, but we will do our best to accommodate you. That's all, thanks,' she said. No groans this time.

* * *

Briefing over, the team departed to their various tasks. Nash sat in her office with Moretti as they went over what was known about the victim. Jared Hussein was in his fifties and married to Hatice Hussein, the lady at the scene with the imam, and who was currently being spoken to by the FLO in the comfort of her own home.

According to Hatice, her husband had been out for the evening in the back room of a house playing cards. He was a gambler who'd ditched the overt attention of the casino for the discreet arena of a small, off-street game. The arrangement she knew about. She wasn't concerned with this. She was concerned about the damage it would cause her family in the eyes of the community. Gambling was frowned upon within her immediate network.

She loved him though, and that's what counted in their marriage of twenty years. Their son, an only child, was devastated at the loss of his decent and caring father. Jared was a regular at the mosque. A well-respected member of the community.

CCTV had corroborated the habitual route he took each Thursday and had done for the last three years.

No one could think of a single person who had fallen out with him. The three occupants of the card school acknowledged he owed no one a penny. Nash had given reassurances to the syndicate, via the detective in attendance, that she was more concerned with the murder than the gambling. Her word was accepted, without question, despite their not knowing her. These were clearly a bunch of men who kept themselves to themselves and fed their habit in a way that caused minimal harm to those close to them. While Nash read through some action sheets, Moretti's mobile phone rang out.

'DS Moretti,' he answered.

'Yes, how much longer? OK, we'll see you there in forty.' He ended the call and put his phone back in his jacket while gathering his belongings together.

'That was the SOCO. They've identified a possible premises the assailant could have been in. Trainer marks at the scene lead from a block of flats to the area he was killed. The marks are very fresh and need a follow-up. There's a search team there ready to start.'

Nash screwed the cap back on her Montblanc fountain pen and placed it in her coat pocket, making sure it was clipped to the internal fabric.

'Best we head off, then. I'll call the search team leader as we travel and let's get a dog down there too.'

With that they headed out to Moretti's work car, relieved in the knowledge they had a starting point from which to work as the body's site had revealed little.

'Stop off at a garage on the way, will you? I'm starving,' Nash said as she pressed her seat belt home.

'Don't you ever eat breakfast?' Moretti asked as he headed for the tiger trap gates that would release them from Hendon and the roads back to the scene.

'Not when a murder breaks, no. I'm just glad I'm still alive and able to eat, Nick,' Nash replied as she sat back in her seat and rubbed her eyes. Eyes tired from too many early mornings and late nights. She smiled at him. 'Let's go and make a difference to his family.'

CHAPTER FOUR

Nash checked her phone messages as she ate a sandwich she'd purchased.

'So how are you enjoying the tour so far?' Nash asked Moretti as she finished the sandwich and reached for the water perched in the central cup holder of the car.

'Oh, just great, Pip. Nothing like having a murder to investigate,' he replied with a smile.

'You do know this has the potential for a major kick-off in the community? A family man, who happens to be Muslim, murdered outside his place of worship. The press

18

won't stop. I've been looking at news sites on the way over. There's lots of chatter about white supremacists being responsible and how an uprising is needed,' Nash said.

Nash sipped her water and took in the sights as they progressed towards Finsbury Park. 'I'll have to do a press statement once we know what we're dealing with. Until then, the Borough Commander can deal with the fallout on the streets. It's his job after all,' she continued.

They returned to the now familiar location in Finsbury Park. Moretti parked their car outside a Victorian terrace. Nash got out and approached the SOCO a short distance from the vehicle. Moretti waited while they chatted. His phone rang and he answered it. After a short while Nash returned to where Moretti was stood outside the cordon of a recreational area.

'Right, it's all a bit clearer now. The SOCO found tiny white pellets of grit. She thought they looked like cat litter but dismissed it at first due to the outside nature of the scene. Then she found similar fragments of the same type near the scene that became discarded across the roadway and on the grass area that's taped off. The last piece she found at the bottom of this block behind us. She believes our killer was watching from up above and when they saw their opportunity they alighted from a balcony and used the cover of the trees to approach the victim. That way they wouldn't look suspicious out in the street or be caught on CCTV hanging around. She found trainer marks in the soil that had similar white grit in the grooves in the earth and they headed away from the block towards where our victim was stabbed. She'll take casts of the indentations so we can match shoeprints should we find our suspect, if they still have the trainers, of course,' Nash said.

Moretti acknowledged the update with a nod.

'I just took a call from George. He's looked at CAD messages of calls to the area and he found one that relates to this block, two hours before the ambulance was called. A Ms Evans contacted the police; she thought she heard someone outside her balcony. It was marked up as non-urgent on the system and it's still outstanding for uniform to deal with. Controller deemed the caller as vague and incoherent when he called her back for more information,' Moretti said.

A sergeant in his forties approached them both – his peak hat set back on his head, blue overalls bedecked with a name badge and three stripes on his epaulettes along with the number 97CO. A sign outside the property saying it was "To Let" had given them the details they needed to contact the estate agents who gave them written permission to do what was required in the circumstances. To Nash, that included removing whatever was deemed of evidential value.

After a quick chat kerbside, the sergeant let them in through the main door. He'd been to get the key. As they ascended the stairs with a posse of uniform and Scenes of Crime Officers, Nash took in the smell of damp. The house was split to accommodate six occupancies from what the doorbell on the outside indicated.

How the agents could describe it as desirable, she'd never understand.

They reached the third floor and Nash opened the door to the flat they first needed to examine. Once they were all suited and gloved, Nash and Moretti waited while the SOCO entered and designated a common approach path on which they could all eventually tread. The agent had been adamant it was unoccupied. A metal fire escape ladder provided access from the ground floor to a balcony that served the room they were in. The accommodation consisted of a living and sleeping area, a small bathroom, and a smaller kitchen that had a single electric oven and a sink. A mattress-less bedframe was out of its wall casing.

'You may want to look at this?' The SOCO motioned for Nash to come over to the door that opened inwards onto a single balcony large enough for a clotheshorse and a few plants. That wasn't what the SOCO was pointing out. Her attention was drawn to the clear line of sight the balcony offered to the entrance of the mosque. A tree provided cover from view from below and across the street.

With the search underway, Nash took the opportunity to knock on a few doors in the block.

Nash wished to speak with the neighbour below and the caller to the police. She gave the customary dot-dash-dash knock, and waited. They didn't have to wait long. An elderly lady came to the door and opened it a crack.

'Yes?' she said. Half a face that had seen many years became visible between the door and the doorframe.

'It's the police. Can we come in and have a word, please?' Nash replied.

'Do you have identification? I'm not letting you in without seeing identification. The crime in this area is atrocious,' she said. Her glaucoma-glazed eye fixed on them through the slit the door provided. They both obliged and waited as the door chain was taken off. Eventually a bespectacled lady with thinning grey hair, in her late eighties, beckoned them in.

'Please mind the cats as they aren't allowed outside, only to the balcony for the litter trays,' she explained as she shuffled towards the rear of the bedsit and what appeared to be a layout that mirrored the flat above in terms of space and outlook. Neither Nash nor Moretti could see any cats.

The smell of damp from the communal area now became a smell of stale urine that obviously inhabited the floral-cloth-covered furniture. Nash walked over to the lady's balcony door and couldn't go further due to the overflowing litter trays that were spread over the outside floor like mosaic tiles. Nash gathered she must let the cats in and out as there was no cat flap. They overflowed with filth and fresh white litter where she'd opened the door and sprinkled it out like rice confetti at a shotgun wedding.

'Would either of you like a tea?' the old dear offered looking between the two.

'No, thank you,' came the reply in unison.

Some places you just didn't accept a drink or sit down, and this was one of them. Nash made a mental note to contact Housing and see what support the lady was receiving. She believed in article eight of the Human Rights Act, but everyone needed support especially when you're advancing in years. She'd been in too many addresses where the vulnerable were left to their own devices and this was one such individual who displayed all the hallmarks of neglect.

'Were you in last night, Mrs…,' Nash tentatively enquired as she looked out the balcony window.

'It's Ms… Ms Evans and yes I was in, dear. I don't get out much now.'

'Did you see or hear anything unusual in the early hours of this morning?'

'Well, as you ask, I haven't been sleeping well at all of late. I thought I heard footsteps from the place above, but I know it's unoccupied, and has been for some time now, so I put it down to the wind or my deteriorating mind,' she answered coherently and assured at what she'd heard.

'Do you remember what time you heard the footsteps?' Nash pressed, delicately.

'Yes, it was at three thirty in the morning. I always need… well, you know, to *go* at around that time so I was awake and getting up.'

'Did you check further to see what it could be?' Moretti asked.

'No. I keep myself to myself and don't get involved in anyone's business but my own. It does remind me, though, that I also heard the sound of someone climbing metal, yes… definitely metal,' she said as she pinched the frame to her glasses that were secured with Sellotape and hope.

She started feeling around a small table that was cluttered with papers. Nash recognised the similarity with her own desk. Ms Evans found a pen and began writing. What she was writing they didn't know, and left her to it. Nash left her to Moretti's questions as she casually looked around the room and outside vista.

The lady slowly got up from the low-sprung chair and made her way towards a closed door. Both Moretti and Nash watched, more out of concern that she could fall in her apparent frailty than anything else. As she opened it, a shower of cats spilled out and began running into the room, rubbing their heads around Moretti's legs and ignoring Nash. The mewing became louder as each moggy expressed its desire for food.

'I'm sorry I can't be of more help,' Ms Evans said as she chirped at her feline friends through pursed lips in an effort to gather them together.

Nash had heard enough. The smell of cat now increased tenfold and she could feel her nose burn from the increased toxicity in the air.

'Well, thank you, Ms Evans; you've been most helpful. We'll leave you to feed your, your–'

'Cats, dear, they're cats,' she interrupted, brusquely.

Nash smiled politely but awkwardly and caught Moretti's eye as he shook a scrawny-looking tabby off his leg.

'Thank you, you've been most helpful,' he said as he followed Nash out shutting the door behind them, all cats and Ms Evans suitably contained.

'Sorry, Nick, but that was doing my head in and I'm allergic to cats,' Nash said as she brushed herself down.

'At least I know to avoid that as a surprise gift,' Moretti said as he led them back upstairs to the top floor.

'It's a disgrace the way we treat the elderly in this country. She must be cared for like a human being should be, not left to be discovered like an Egyptian pharaoh, mummified by maggots, surrounded by dead cats,' Nash completed her social observation now they were outside the top room's door.

'Ah, you're back,' the search sergeant exclaimed, hacked off at the wait. 'The SOCO wants a chat.'

They re-entered the flat and were shown towards where the SOCO stood near the doorway to the balcony.

'This may or may not be of interest, Inspector, but I'm showing you nonetheless,' the SOCO said as she massaged her gloved hands together.

Nash kept her hands to herself and just observed and listened as the SOCO continued.

'I'm beginning to think our suspect may have found the downstairs balcony first and trodden in cat faeces and litter as the trays cover the whole floor area. They've then climbed up here as there's less chance of being disturbed and we have concentrations of cat litter on the floor and metal steps of the fire escape that lead down to floor level,' she said.

As Nash looked out from the flat's large window across the balcony, she saw that the crowd present earlier that morning had increased, flowers now forming a shrine.

Nash finished speaking with the search team and they left to drop the keys in at the agency.

CHAPTER FIVE

They'd both attended the post mortem before coming back to the Peel Centre. The conclusion reached by the examination didn't come as a surprise and was as they'd both expected. The victim died from a cut to the throat that severed the jugular. Death would have been quick. A sense of relief for both of them as they hated to think he'd had to suffer any more trauma than he had.

As their vehicle approached the gates, Nash couldn't help but notice security was tighter than normal.

They joined a line of cars waiting to gain access. The alert state board had been changed from amber to red and the usual civilian security guard on the gate had been replaced with two armed cops. A clear message that somewhere, the shit had hit the fan. A critical incident, significant enough that the base was considered a potential target. From whom or why they didn't know. Moretti rolled the car up to the barrier that prevented them going any further and an armed officer stepped forward.

Moretti lowered the window.

'Hi, can I see some ID please?' the uniform officer asked as he bent forward so Moretti could see him. He stood an open door's distance from the car so he could level his MP5 quickly and get off a shot should he need to.

'DS Moretti from the murder team, MIT 2. We work here, what's going on?' he said, handing his warrant card over to be checked.

'There's been a threat of attack by an extremist group following the murder in Finsbury Park. Every station has upped their game, it's fucking chaos,' the cop replied.

Moretti took his warrant card back and pocketed it. 'That's a bummer. Well, hopefully it will all get resolved quickly,' he replied.

The cop nodded at his colleague who raised the barrier. Moretti drove on, found a space, and parked up. He cut the engine.

'A bummer? Is that the best you could come up with?' Nash said.

Moretti took off his glasses and rubbed his eyes. The weight of the dark bold frames had caused a red indentation on the bridge of his nose.

Nash continued, 'How do we know it isn't a terrorist incident? It could be a right-wing extremist group who haven't claimed responsibility yet. I've notified the Anti-Terrorist lot and they're maintaining a watching brief. If we start down a false trail, then the rest of the team do too. Until a group comes forward claiming they killed Mr Hussein, then we carry on as we are. I don't believe any group is responsible. The victim, by all accounts so far, is just a regular guy who happened to like his cards and practised a faith. I don't like the idea of some lone wolf out there taking liberties with the community any more than you do. Until we've established who it is, we have to work through the shitstorm that's started building, methodically and meticulously, until we get answers. So, "yeah, it's a bummer" isn't the best response right now.' Nash got out the car.

Moretti grabbed his folder and walked alongside her towards the rear entrance to their office.

As they got close to the building, Moretti stopped under a covered entrance to the main door. 'Go ahead, I need a smoke then I'll be up. I'm sorry for the flippant remark. I'll organise the team for a briefing in twenty minutes,' he said.

Nash nodded and left him to it.

* * *

He loaded up the bowl to his pipe and waved a Zippo over the strips of leaf until it sparked to life. The red glow of the tobacco and the exhalation of smoke told him it had hit the spot. He wasn't a regular smoker but at this time in his life he'd become accustomed to the minimal comfort breaks it gave him.

He also relished the timeout it supplied for him to think.

Moretti was aware of the time pressures building up. He remained outside for fifteen minutes then took one last draw and tapped out the residue from the wooden bowl. He knew she had it all under control and, as Nash's DS, he felt a duty to ensure he kept it that way. He put the pipe away and entered the office building.

* * *

Nash entered the incident room. A room that accommodated her HOLMES team and intelligence desk – the inside team, as they were known. Nash had a permanent incident room. It was the one she was standing in now, looking at her detectives and police staff as they tapped away at keyboards or sat and read statements. There was never a requirement to set up a fresh incident room – just set up a new board and off they went.

She kept the meeting informal. Each officer sat at their respective desk while Nash perched on the edge of a spare one. Her blue counsel's notebook, or daybook as it was known, on her lap ready to make notes. She noticed Moretti was back and called the room to order and began.

'Where are we with the CCTV?' she asked, looking at DC Squires.

Squires peered over the rim of his glasses. 'I've taken some footage from a private camera system in a residential house down to the lab to see if we can clean it up. The camera overlooked the green area where the fire escape ladder was. I'm not hopeful. It was a cheap system and the outside image is grainy due to a poor night-vision camera. I was hoping it may reveal our suspect once it's been cleaned up,' he said.

'Thanks. OK, what about the victim's family?'

The FLO looked up, her finger acting as a bookmark in a page in her contact log. 'The main concern is the funeral arrangements. I've offered what support we can, and Mrs Hussein is appreciative of all we're doing. What we know about the victim has already been covered and nothing has surfaced to contradict that. Not much more to add, I'm afraid,' she said.

'I'll let you know as soon as the body can be released for burial. It shouldn't be much longer now. Once Dr King and I are satisfied all forensic opportunity has been established without the need to re-examine the victim, then his body will be released,' Nash said, allowing a pause before she continued.

'I've also had notification of a list of UK-manufactured hunting knives. I'll get Intel desk to work those up. See if we can get an idea of what type of blade could cause the wound going on the details supplied by Dr King. With any luck we'll be able to trace the weapon if it's been used in another offence that's come to police notice, as it's a needle in a haystack situation at the moment. The SOCO will run the trainer lifts and see if that turns up anything useful. I appreciate we still haven't got much to go on but keep up the good work and let's hope we get a breakthrough soon.

'As always, get your actions returned to George as quickly as you can and take any new ones he allocates with the same haste. Keep your phones on and stay in touch. Unless there's anything else, get back to it and I'll be in touch should any lead reveal itself.'

* * *

Nash's desk was hidden under a mountain of actions that had been completed and returned. It reminded her of the old woman's table but without the smell of cat. It also jogged her memory to call the social services about Ms Evan's living conditions.

Copies of statements attached to the action forms and other random intelligence feeds supplied from various police departments and open source media begged her attention. The team briefing had gone as expected in these early stages of the investigation. Statements taken, CCTV seized now being viewed, and the FLO doing well to hold the family together. Lab work was being drip-fed for forensic evaluation.

She sat back in her seat, cleared a section of her desk, kicked off her shoes and put her feet up as she took the first document, from the top of Paper Mountain, to read. House-to-house had been what she expected – a poor return. She'd have her team on that side of the office back out again after they'd eaten, as many people would have returned from work now or be more receptive to answering the door.

The photographer had left digital prints of both scenes on her desk. She put down the statement she'd started and picked up the album and flicked through. She stopped at the image of the playing card, holding it in front of her. She placed it on the desk and continued looking at it. Nothing. There were no gambling debts owed that warranted Hussein's death, no enemies to speak of at all. He just played cards and looked after his family and she hoped his faith now looked after Hatice and his son.

Her mind went back to the crime scene and the image of his body laid out on the pavement; face crumpled into railings as though he was desperate to look through. An empty form downed like a puppet with its strings severed. The river of blood that had painted the cement and mixed in with the grime of the street filled her frontal lobe. Nash had hoped that part of her brain would make the image more palatable. After all the bodies she'd witnessed in death, it was still wishful thinking, she realised.

She'd worked plenty of shooting scenes. Inevitably the outside ones were tough for forensic value. The best killers consider their trade a skillset worthy of forensic study and increased awareness. This wasn't the usual knife crime case.

At least with them there's a possibility of a registration number, or someone in the community willing to talk. The dog handler who'd attended the scene had lost the track, and put this down to the suspect having a vehicle to abscond in laid up nearby. With that thought, she put down the picture of the playing card and decided to take a walk to the source unit that served her team. A unit that recruited and handled informants or Covert Human Intelligence Sources, CHIS, for short.

The CHIS unit consisted of a small band of hermit type cops who spent their days secreted behind a locked door. Either they were on phones, on a computer, or outside with criminals on the street. Much of what they were told by their sources was accurate and worthy of police action. Their role was undervalued, and the subject of much scorn and derision by some officers who didn't appreciate it due to its secrecy and covert nature. Without a product or arrest, the source didn't get paid. The hardest part for the handlers was convincing people like Nash that their source wasn't the triggerman or involved more than they let on.

She rapped on the door and waited. She could hear the shuffle of a chair then footsteps. A swarthy-looking DC greeted her, late forties, silver hair. Nash had given him the nickname "the Silverfox" as he had a shifty manner after many years working the harsher end of the streets.

'Second job?' Nash enquired as she was offered over the threshold to their compact and secure office. The security door closed behind her creating a solid seal.

The Silverfox was dressed in a pair of paint-splattered denims and a plaid shirt. All items of clothing appeared to have been on the same decorating venture. His trainers had suffered a similar fate; as had his hands. All designed to fit in with the theatre.

Nash availed herself of the first seat she could find. A board opposite her displayed initials only. No full names were used here, even the initials denoted a pseudonym not true ID. Everything was in one code or another, such was the professionalism to keep those who assisted the police anonymous.

'This?' He motioned at his attire with his hands. 'No, part of a cover story for a guy we're working with right now. Good fella, well connected, especially where guns and shootings are concerned. Anyway, how can I help you, Pip?'

Nash accepted first-name terms with these boys as that's the way they operated. They never used police terminology on the street. To do so would blow the covert role they performed. Everyone, regardless of rank, was referred to by their first name and if they didn't like it, they could take a walk.

Nash valued the input they gave as she'd done the role as a DC. Not at the same level as these guys but a basic grassroots "meet and greet then handover" role. Many a murder investigation had been given a boost by information from one of their sources that eventually led Nash and her team towards the final goal. She hoped they'd be able to assist in this one.

'I take it you've heard about the murder in the early hours of this morning?' she asked.

'I have. We've put the word out, but so far, it's a blank. No gang we know is claiming responsibility and from what we've heard, it sounds calculated and not a gang execution,' the Silverfox replied.

'You're right.'

'Coffee?' the Silverfox asked, as Nash heard a kettle click.

'That'd be great,' she replied. She got up to take the offered mug and looked out over the parade square through the slatted blinds. 'What is the word on the street?'

The handler took a sip and put his mug down. He moved back to the fridge, opened the door, and took out the milk.

'Cancel coffee, milk's off,' he said as he put the two mugs down and re-boiled the kettle. Nash accepted the freshly made black coffee with grace as the handler sat back down opposite her, legs outstretched, looking like any other decorator in London on a comfort break.

'To be honest, there's nothing. Everyone we've spoken to is as shocked as we are about it. People we have in that area all say he was a decent bloke. His whole family is respected, not a criminal bone in his body.' He paused. 'He liked to gamble, lost a shit load of money once at a casino uptown but since then he'd learnt to downsize his expectations so was part of a card school in someone's

31

back room. The house they used is close to the mosque. I can find out where if that would help?'

'We've covered that, thanks, and confirmed what you're hearing. Anything else you can get to build a bigger picture would be appreciated. Associates too,' she replied.

'You don't fancy a return to covert policing, do you? We could do with a boss like you. Ours is a diamond, but he's retiring and the names in the hat are appalling,' the Silverfox said.

Nash smiled. 'My want for twenty-four-hour days are well and truly over. I'll take the short bursts this job comes with but not the constant demand you lot are under. No, thank you,' she replied as she downed the last dregs and set the mug on a vacant desk.

'Thank the other three for all they're doing. I've seen what's coming in upstairs for other jobs and I appreciate the efforts you've all gone to on many of our enquiries,' Nash added as the DC gave a mock salute.

She left and waved her phone as she exited. Their code to get hold of her as soon as something came in.

CHAPTER SIX

Nash checked her watch. 7 p.m. It had been a long and brutal day but not as brutal as it had been for the victim's family. She remembered that as she shuffled through the list of actions that had been returned to be signed off. The landing they worked from was quiet save for the light tapping of keyboards from the few inside team members that remained in the office opposite.

She'd sent some of the staff home as their services could wait until morning and she had a budget to manage too. She gave the hours required to get the job done and left the assassination, for want of a better word, for Moretti to face when the DCI saw the bill at the end of the year. She'd given him the joint responsibility as part of his annual performance indicators. She'd take the flak too, but thought it would be good to give him the chance at the same experience as her of defending officer overtime when the DCI would complain about it.

The job would always find the cash from someone else's budget that didn't deserve the amount they were allocated in the first place. If it wasn't about figures for detections and reductions in crime, then it was all about money spent to achieve them or the computer strokes employed to reduce them.

All of which didn't concern DI Pippa Nash. Her job was clear: assume nothing, believe no one, and challenge everything. The ABCs of the detective. She heard the office door bang and turned to see the two cleaners. One trailing a Henry vacuum cleaner and a garland of bin bags looped into his jeans. He started collecting the rubbish from each metal bin, replacing the bags and draping spares over the edge. Nice touch, Nash thought, as she was sick of trying to locate them whenever the main bin became too full. He deftly cleared the room nodding his head to whatever he was listening to through his Beats over-ear headphones.

The other cleaner wiped down the available desk surfaces they could access. Moretti strode back in and broke her train of thought.

'Anything new?' Moretti enquired as the cleaners exited. The hoover smashing into the doorframe as it was dragged out on its wheels.

'Nada, nothing. It's as though this killer was a ghost,' Nash replied as she stretched her arms over her head and sat.

Moretti looked away, giving her some space.

She unclipped the wooden hair comb that held her hair in place and relaxed into the feeling of freedom it gave her as her honey blonde hair cascaded below her shoulders.

'Call it a night, Pip. I'll contact you if anything breaks overnight. I'll have the team rally back at 08:00 tomorrow. We can pick up where we left off and see what we're missing,' Moretti said.

Nash acknowledged the offer her DS had made but she had other plans as she collected her handbag.

'I appreciate the concern, Nick, but I'm going back to the scene to see how house-to-house are getting on,' she said.

CHAPTER SEVEN

Midnight. The end of a long day and the sixty-second pause before a new one. Moretti parked up the job car and grabbed his brown leather jacket and grab bag from the passenger seat. He never risked leaving anything police-related in full view. The stab proof vest and first aid kit remained in the boot and he hoped would be there with his car when he returned in the morning.

Vehicle theft was a major issue in this part of the marina along with burglary, robbery, and drug dealing. This was London after all. He strode back towards his barge looking forward to the final collapse into bed. That thought was soon an illusion. He clocked the distinctive fiery red glow of a cigarette tip from the outside space of his boat. He didn't need to change path, as the minimal lighting on the approach road wasn't illuminating him.

He had two options: enter the barge from his usual entrance way at the front of the boat or take one at the rear of the boat furthest from his uninvited guest. He opted for the latter. He was carrying his ASP and racked the mechanism. The metal pole shot out from the handle housing and securely locked in place. The weight felt good in his hand.

He ditched his bag near the barge and crept slowly towards the figure. Another red dot shone through and in the dim light he could make out the person was wearing a parka. The hood was up. The faux fur lining masked the wearer's face. The uninvited guest was also wearing black leather gloves. Moretti was aware this could be the lookout and an accomplice could be inside going through his stuff. Not much worth taking, in Moretti's mind, as he enjoyed a minimalist lifestyle, and the occasional guest he invited back often commented that he must have just moved in and not unpacked.

He considered his next move as he paused. Moretti was a textbook example of a cop who would exercise restraint when he was detached from the situation. This situation was personal though. Detachment didn't come into the equation; this was his home. Gone were any thoughts of losing his rank or job. He wanted justice. Swift. Effective. Street-style justice. He stayed low. The suspect's back towards him. He took a deep breath then launched himself at the figure. As he leapt the barge must have moved slightly as the suspect now turned to see Moretti in full leap. He raised the ASP high above his head, one foot in the air as he yelled, 'Stay where you are! Police officer.'

It was all done and dusted in a flash as Moretti landed on top of the figure. They briefly rolled then stopped. Tabatha screamed at him as she beat him on his back with open hands. Moretti released his hold and sat up. Tabatha pulled the hood from her face. The situation calmed in an instant as she lit a match and held it in front where Moretti could see.

They sat still for a moment then burst into laughter. Moretti got up and with an offered hand pulled her onto her feet. The ASP was still racked and would remain so as the only way to collapse it back into the handle was to hit the ball end against something solid. He needed concrete for that. There was no way he'd use any part of the boat.

'What in the hell are you doing on my boat at this time?' Moretti quizzed Tabatha as they made their way inside.

'Having a smoke, clearing my head. My boat's too small to sit outside and I figured you were out and wouldn't mind... sorry,' she replied. She dumped her parka on the kitchen chair.

Tabatha was a blonde with a roll and sway body. She was a stripper by profession and a good one at that. At least that's what she'd told him when he first moved to the marina and she'd dropped by on her way back from a night shift. He was up top on the barge where she'd just been, having a small bowl of smoking tobacco from an ornamental opium pipe he'd picked up at a charity shop.

Tabatha had stayed and chatted all about her life. She was keen to assert that she wasn't a prostitute but enjoyed the dance, money, and some of the attention. She enlightened him as to the diverse community he'd chosen to live among: bankers, young couples, babies, marrieds, the old, and those who simply couldn't live conventionally.

Tonight, she was dressed in dark yoga pants and matching T-shirt. She wore the clothes well but looked cold. Moretti went to the fridge, taking out an opened bottle of Prosecco and poured two glasses. He handed her one, and they went through to the living room.

'You got any matches left?' he asked.

'Yeah, here.' She threw Moretti the box. He set alight the wood in the burner he'd prepared days ago but never lit. The fire took hold, and he joined her on the brown leather three-seat sofa that was a feature in the living room. They each occupied one end but were comfortable enough with their feet up in the middle.

'I heard about the murder over the river. It's all over the local news. Fucking nasty that one,' she said as Moretti took a drink.

'Certainly was. Were you working tonight?' Moretti enquired deflecting the conversation away from his work; this was his time to wind down.

'Day off. Just stayed here. Couldn't face Christmas shopping. I'm broke and need the cash for the mooring fees next year,' she said as she took a drink and savoured the warmth the alcohol gave.

'What got you into stripping in the first place?' Moretti asked not knowing whether it was appropriate or not, but was genuinely interested to know.

'Necessity. I'm an artist by trade but can't make ends meet on that alone. A mate who did it told me of the money she was making. She introduced me to a club owner and I've just got used to it now, I guess. I make a good amount on a busy night, in tips – money tips I'm talking about. I've heard you coppers have filthy minds and I've seen many with such minds in the club too.' She smiled.

Moretti smiled back. He could think of a few on his team that would be prime suspects.

'Never had you down for one of them. A copper, I mean. You're different… keep yourself to yourself all alone on a boat big enough for a family of ten. Why's that then?' she asked, as Moretti refilled his glass. Hers wasn't empty but she accepted the refill.

'Because that's the way I like it. Same as you. By the end of a shift I've had enough drama, responsibility, and taking on other people's shit. I just want to be alone in my own space, my own little world.' He stared into the wood burner, shocked at his own acceptance that that was how it was for him. One of the reasons it never worked out with any relationship he ventured into. He was never there, never present.

'Sorry. It's been a long day and I'm not at my most sociable,' he said by way of explanation. He turned back to Tabatha who now lay curled into the arm of the settee, eyes shut, mouth opened to reveal the tiniest split between her dark red lips. He moved towards her and out of instinct felt her wrist. Her pulse beat steadily; she was asleep.

He put it down to the time of night, the warmth of the fire, and that she'd been drinking before he'd arrived. She wasn't drunk but had had enough that the wine had taken its full effect. Moretti found a blanket and a pillow and after taking off her shoes, he placed the cushion under her head. She stirred but remained passive as he covered her prone body with the blanket he would use on a rainy day when he enjoyed curling up and reading. He took the glasses and switched off the light.

He needed sleep and fast. He wondered what would have been if she'd stayed awake. Probably nothing, he thought as he shut the door to his bedroom.

Moretti undressed, collapsed into bed, and closed his eyes.

CHAPTER EIGHT

Moretti stirred. His alarm had been sounding its call to arms for a while and he'd slept through it. He palmed down the *off* button on the top of the radio alarm clock that occupied his bedside cabinet. It showed 07:30. He'd done it again. Overslept.

His phone buzzed, and a text hit his screen. It was from Nash.

*In office, will do briefing. Team cakes on your way in
and shift your arse. N.*

It was as though she knew he wouldn't be there this
morning. He ruffled his hair and sat up. He was
disappointed in himself that he'd let her down and would
buy cakes for the team as recompense for his poor
performance, and a bottle of her favourite vodka as an
apology. But in his mind, there was little time-sensitive
evidence to go on. Despite the brutality of the murder the
forensic evidence was weak. The other standard practices
of any investigation were proving slow to gain enough
momentum to be reacted to.

He took a shower and got dressed. As he entered the
kitchen area, he could smell toast and remembered he had
a guest. Tabatha was up and had put the kettle on. Two
mugs graced the counter, a tea bag in each. He didn't own
a matching set. He hadn't found one in a charity shop yet.

'Morning. Sleep well?' Moretti asked feeling thankful he
hadn't wandered out scratching his balls while looking for
a glass of water.

'Like a log. So sorry I fell asleep like that. I don't
normally pass out when I have good company and decent
wine. I haven't been sleeping well as the heating's off on
my boat and can't be repaired until next week.' She let that
hang in the air as she poured boiling water into the mugs
and accepted the toast Moretti had buttered.

'Oh, I get it now, so last night was about needing a
place to crash rather than freeze to death in a fridge for a
boat?' He smiled and she reciprocated his warmth from
behind the mug she held up to her lips, cradled with both
hands. Her eyes lit up.

He felt like he had little option as she leant against the
work surface, barelegged save for the long T-shirt that
came down above her knees. She must have woken in the
night and stripped down. The heat from the fire would
have been enough for her to want to do that. He liked her,

there was no hiding that fact, but he'd have let her stay, anyway. She had a fresh outlook on life that he enjoyed seeing. She was relaxed and gave off an aura of being carefree. A far cry from the formality of his own life. A life governed by legislation and internal policy. He decided to put her mind at rest as he needed to be in work.

'You can crash here; there's a spare room. No parties, guests, or drugs. Other than that, the place is yours,' Moretti said as he retrieved a spare key from the utensil drawer and handed it to her. As he did, she leaned into him and kissed his cheek, the warmth of her mouth an enjoyable comfort.

'Thank you, it means a lot. I won't get in your way, promise,' she said as she went back into the living area.

Moretti grabbed his coat, keys, and remembered the grab bag he'd left last night. He went out the main door to the barge and closed it behind him.

The fresh air embraced his face with a slap as the chill hit his lungs. He paused, turned back, and opened the boat's door.

'I'm off to work, help yourself to whatever you need,' he said into the void.

'Thanks, I'll get some food in later from my boat so don't worry on that count… oh and booze,' came the reply.

As Moretti started shutting the boat's main door, he heard her say, 'Stay safe.'

* * *

Nash was finishing off a telephone call as Moretti strolled past the door to the main incident room. She clocked him and waved him in.

'Yes, of course… well we can live in hope, eh? Thank you,' Nash said as she replaced the receiver.

Moretti hesitated at her door and entered carrying a large brown box. He placed it on her desk and looking behind him first, retrieved a bottle of vodka from his bag and handed it to her.

'I'm sorry, Pip, I should have been here and I feel terrible to have overslept when we've a live job running. I hope the cakes and the token bottle will be enough to show how embarrassed I am,' he said, as he shuffled his feet.

Nash took the bottle, opened her desk drawer and added it to three others that occupied the melamine base. She opened the lid of the box and retrieved a chocolate éclair. She sat back and took a bite before responding to Moretti, who by now was wishing the ground would open up and take him with it.

She pointed at Moretti with the bitten end.

'Wake up, Nick, and get a grip. That lot out there are looking to me and you to lead them and if my DS fails to appear at a morning briefing then it sends the wrong message. I just hope she was worth it,' she said as Moretti attempted to close the lid on the cakes but his hand was slapped as he did.

'I trust you bought more than required,' she said as she took an apple turnover.

He sat down opposite her.

'Was that good news?' he asked in reference to her call before she'd collared him.

'It was Intel; they don't have a match on a knife from the details provided from Dr King.' Nash paused then continued, 'So, we're no further forward. Could be a military connection to access that type of clean blade, or someone medically trained, or someone who hunts. The list goes on. I'm no expert on military kit and from what I have seen on the news they're lucky to get a rifle let alone a tactical knife of some kind. We'd better do some checks with the MOD though and the hospitals, see if they've had anything stolen or go missing that they're keeping quiet about that could produce a surgically clean cut.'

It had to be worth trying. With the right contacts, anyone could access serious weaponry and the military weren't exempt. She addressed Moretti again as another thought surfaced.

'Do we know if the victim or his associates have any military or medical connections?'

'Not yet, but I very much doubt it. All research is coming back clean as a whistle. He only seems to travel to Dubai and when he does, he takes his family with him. He hasn't been travelling to any countries that would be of concern to our colleagues in the Anti-Terrorist branch,' he replied.

'OK. If that's leading nowhere then we'll sit down and reassess where to widen the search parameters,' she suggested, Moretti nodding in agreement.

Moretti retired to the incident room and those left in the office cheered at the sight of him carrying a cake box. He set it down near the kettle and shrugged by way of apology. He'd rather be within the main engine room, but he knew he'd get nothing done there with all the distractions; plus, the staff could relax when his rank wasn't among them. He knew they respected him as a DS and rated his ability, but he also respected their space as they did his. Boundaries were a necessity in order to function effectively.

Nash managed an hour before she needed to take a thinking break. She was about to head outside when the Silverfox knocked on her door. She beckoned him in, and the handler sat down.

'I hope you've come to tell me you've wrapped this job up in a pretty bow and we can all go home?' she asked, raising her eyebrows.

'I wish. No such luck, I'm afraid, but we took a call last night about a guy who's dealing cocaine–'

Nash raised her hand, cutting the handler short. 'I've got no capacity to drop on to one of your drug jobs, as much as I'd love to,' she said, knowing the Silverfox would appreciate the joke.

'Well, that'd be a first.' The handler laughed then continued, 'I thought you'd want to know as this dealer also has a penchant for military memorabilia: rifles, bayonets, clothing, that type of thing. He lives opposite the mosque; our source also reckons there were cops all over a house opposite and he phoned us thinking you'd raided the wrong address, as the fella they know is always getting turned over,' he said, hoping his source was correct as the ribbing Nash and her team would give him for misinformation would be relentless.

'What else is your source alluding to?' Nash asked.

'Look, Pip, I can tell you as you're sound and know the score. He's seen a knife that he described as futuristic-looking but lethal. Totally legit and not some film prop.' The Silverfox looked around as he imparted the provenance.

Nash's ears pricked.

'Why didn't you call me last night?'

'I didn't call because the knife wasn't there. Source says it was out on loan but coming back tonight as the fella in the flat has loaded up with gear and is looking to start getting rid of it, so he wanted his protection close to him.'

'How reliable is this source of yours? And before you start, don't give me the usual patter about them being the best in the Met; I'm not in the mood for getting the runaround. I'm up against the clock here,' Nash said.

'Shit. Look, Pip, they're good. Been on the books for many years, always comes up with the goods. The friendly is out to earn so when they say it's there, it'll be there.' The handler sat back with a wry smile on his face.

Nash knew exactly what that look conveyed. It wasn't unknown for an informant to set things up in order to get paid.

'I don't want to know any more. That's for you to manage. I'll react to whatever you tell me. By that I mean

I'll do what needs doing no matter what comes back on forensics. If that means your source's dabs are all over a gun or drugs, then he gets lifted too. Put the information through the usual channels to my team for action. Sanitise it to read, "the occupant at", wherever they live, "has access to a firearm and is dealing cocaine". The suspect will be used to that. I don't want him thinking we're focussing on a knife, not at this stage. He can own as many knives as he likes in his house. You'll have the full provenance and information on your secure system, obviously. I'll need that for disclosure, but it won't see court, only our prosecutor at a pre-trial review. That will do for me,' Nash said as she stood up indicating the meeting was over. She patted him on the shoulder on his way out.

'I hope this plays out or it will cost you dearly in drinks at the wrap party,' she said.

'It'll be sound, Pip. Trust me.'

'I'll never do that,' Nash replied with a smile.

CHAPTER NINE

'OK, everyone, can I have your attention please, thank you.' Nash brought the room to order. She'd gathered the team for a midday briefing and update from the morning's work. They ran through CCTV, house-to-house, and forensics, none of which moved them forward. Nash turned her attention to the intelligence desk, and an analyst ran through various information logs that had been entered on the CRIMINT system – the database used for storing and sharing information on criminals and suspected criminals.

Another analyst waved a single sheet of A4 aloft. From the light passing through the cheap printer paper Nash could see it contained a single sentence.

'This came through earlier, ma'am. Its origin remains classified, but it states that the occupant of 6c Barnfield House has access to a firearm. It's flagged to you for action,' the analyst announced.

'Well, no guessing where that's come from,' a DC said from across the meeting table.

Ripples of laughter echoed through the room. Nash was just as amused. There are lengths the job will go to for information to appear to be random and not from an informant but there are also times where it will be obvious to those in the know. Now being one of them.

'Yeah, yeah. So, it's from our source unit and we will be actioning this today,' Nash explained decisively as the jovial nature of the room subsided to moaning and the shuffle of paper and chairs.

'Look, guv, with all the will in the world, they're always coming up with stuff that never amounts to anything more than us lot rushing around on a wild goose chase,' the same truculent DC chipped in.

Nash tolerated him. He was a grafter despite his habitual need to put down any suggestion made in relation to whatever enquiry the team happened to have picked up. Nash's tactic in dealing with him was to ignore him and move on.

'Intel team, get the address and any occupant linked to it worked up. I want any children or dogs who live or frequent the premises highlighted and I'll need a floor plan. I'll be speaking with the Violent Crime Task Force and getting them on-board to raid the address. Nick, you and I will go and see what comes out of it.' Nash signalled the meeting was over by collecting her blue notebook off the desk and gathering up the papers she'd been handed.

The DC who loved the sound of his own voice waited while the others left, then approached her.

'Look, boss. I'm sorry for speaking out, I know I have a habit of doing it, but I mean nothing by it. If I can help, I will,' he said apologetically.

Nash nodded her appreciation at the approach. 'Good. You can help by getting us an observation point overlooking the target address. You can cover the post until we go through the door. I need to know the place is occupied before we hit it. You've a knack at remaining focussed when a job's mundane and I need that skill more than anything now. I must have a prisoner rather than a manhunt and lots of property. Too many exhibits clogging up police property stores with no one charged with possession,' she said as the DC nodded his agreement before leaving.

'Let's hope we get a result,' Moretti said as he walked with Nash towards the canteen.

Moretti admired her for the way she got a job done. Many would have raided the address whether someone was in or not. As the double doors to the canteen opened, cheers resounded as a cop dropped his tray of food on the floor.

They grabbed some food, coffees, and found a vacant table, smiling and nodding at familiar faces as they went.

'So, what are the chances of getting a result today?' Moretti asked Nash when they were settled.

'Depends what you class as a result,' she responded, sniffing her coffee before sipping it.

'Well, the kind of result that means a name on a charge sheet.'

Nash looked at him as she raised a forkful of pasta.

'Slim to none. I can't afford to discount the information, especially as we're getting nothing else coming in. How's the CCTV work coming on?'

'Nothing as yet, other than the grainy footage we're getting enhanced. We've got coverage of the victim getting cut and hitting the deck, but the angle of the camera is poor to identify the suspect as he was hooded and wore a face shield. The knife appears very dark too, no glint off the blade. The blade must be a decent length as he didn't need to hang around. We're doing all we can to gauge the blade size from the footage. I can tell you it isn't a scalpel. Judging by the cut, the blade is at least six inches long and not serrated. It was a decent enough size to span the neck without having to hack away at it. He killed him very quickly. There was no moving traffic by pedestrians or cars when he dropped to the ground. The suspect runs away and disappears from view. They're not picked up again as there's no camera coverage in the street they were in. It also confirms what the imam said in terms of him seeing the body after the murder,' he replied.

Nash set her cutlery down and looked at him.

'How long have you known that the knife used wasn't a scalpel?' she enquired as Moretti shifted in his seat.

'Two hours. I got a call from Owen on the Intel desk,' he said as he rubbed his chin.

'Did you not consider I needed to know that crucial piece of information? Information I needed to know in case we recover a suspect and search for the weapon? Information I could've imparted to the team at the last briefing? That Owen probably wonders why I didn't?' Nash sat back and pushed her plate away no longer hungry.

Moretti grimaced at his further lack of judgment. 'I fucked up, I'm sorry,' he said.

Nash leaned across the table in a way that could be considered an invasion of personal space.

'Sorry won't cut it, Nick. Neither will another bottle of cheap vodka. You either ship up or ship out. I don't care how far back we go, you're becoming a liability and I don't need a DS to babysit, I need a DS to do his fucking job,' she hissed as she sat back and smiled at the approach of DI Drake from the Violent Crime Task Force who'd entered the canteen and was scanning the room to see if he knew anyone while looking for a seat.

Nash caught his attention and DI Drake weaved his way through the tables and chairs.

Finally, he reached their table and took a seat.

'Hi, Pip, long time no see, have I come over at a bad time?' he said as he looked at Moretti's face.

'All good, John, thanks. This is my DS, Nick Moretti,' she said before going into her pitch for resources.

'Actually, I could do with your team's help today. Got intel on an address that could be linked to our murder, but I don't want to show my hand early. I could do with your team making it look like an ordinary drug bust until I'm certain he's our man. Chance of a gun, drugs and our murder weapon if we're lucky,' Nash said as DI Drake rubbed his robust jaw. He had a habit of letting a request sink in before making any commitment.

'As it's you, I think I may be able to provide the troops. They're all here on mandatory training. I'm certain they'd relish a change of scene,' he said as Nash nodded her thanks.

'That'd be great. I'll make sure the briefing is done and sent across to you. If I could leave it with you to organise the firearms side?' she asked.

'Done. I'll get a coffee to go and let the team know they won't be off early. I'm on this number when you're ready.' Drake handed Nash a business card with the Metropolitan Police crest on bearing his rank and contact details.

'All a bit posh, John? I can't get these for my lot for love nor money,' Nash said as she turned it over in her fingers.

'That's because you're not flavour of the month, mate. Murder never was a popular thing for the Commissioner but a unit tackling violent crime in the capital is,' he replied, smiling as he got up.

'Nick will buy your drink, just tell the cashier,' Nash said as Drake went to the posh coffee area.

'Right, let's get back to work, shall we?' she said to Moretti who was busy checking his wallet for cash.

'I didn't think we'd stopped?' Moretti replied as they gathered up their trays, depositing them on a trolley as they left the canteen and headed back to their office.

CHAPTER TEN

Nash waited for the officers' voices to reduce to a murmur then she began her briefing. It was a larger contingent, due to the firearms and DI Drake's teams joining them.

'OK, good people, listen in. The target, and only occupant of the premises, is Lee Brown: white male, six feet in height, practised mixed martial arts when he wasn't dealing drugs. He has no kids or pets that live with him. He's previously been arrested for threatening behaviour during a right-wing protest in the city but denied being a member of the English Defence League despite being among the group when they were stopped and searched. Wrong place wrong time was his defence.' A series of laughs broke through the room.

'DI Drake has assigned his team roles and responsibilities. This will be an armed entry. No one is to move towards the premises until it's declared safe by the firearm tactical advisor. I will relay the message to DI Drake once it's safe for his team to enter. Everyone's to make sure they have their own personal protective equipment with them, and on their person, prior to getting in the cars. Any questions?' Nash looked around the room and there was a unanimous silence.

'Let's do this. Stay safe and watch each other's backs,' she said, and DI Drake indicated by way of a nod that he had nothing further to add. The officers broke away, gathered up their kit, and exited the building.

The parade square at Hendon became a car park when it wasn't in use for a parade or practice marches. Much of the afternoon had been taken up with preparation for the raid. At this late hour it was empty save for the firearms team's cars and those of the Violent Crime Task Force. Firearms officers checked their weapons and shut the boots of their vehicles once they were satisfied everything was as they'd left it when they parked up.

Everyone knew where to go. From here they would attend a forward rendezvous point outside Holloway Police station before they hit the target address. They would only move off once every unit was accounted for. If someone had had an accident on the way, then they'd have to reassign or consider aborting the strike. Engines started up and various headlights lit up the outside of the MIT block. Nash and Moretti were in her car.

'All set?' Nash asked.

'Let's do this,' he replied as Nash got on the radio.

'All units move out to RVP, over.' On her word, blue lights illuminated the parade square as the marked cars came to life.

The convoy headed to the open barrier close to the carwash bay. A uniformed PC in a yellow jacket stepped out to stop traffic and ensure that they could exit as one team. Sirens were activated in unison as each vehicle tipped out of the base towards the A406 and Holloway.

Nash kept up with the lead marked car that burnt up the road towards their destination. She was on a high as she pushed the accelerator and watched the needle rotate clockwise on the speedometer. She was in control and making good progress. Moretti sat back and enjoyed the thrill of the ride. He watched the houses and cars as they evaporated into streams of light trails as they motored past.

Nash had taken a call earlier in the day from her DCI about the progress, or lack of it, with the investigation. The DCI was concerned that the heat was rising from simmer to boil as the press and community demanded results. Nash explained she was working with all she had. The DCI took that in the spirit it was meant, to back off. She knew her role, and this wasn't her first enquiry where someone had been murdered. Nash appreciated the Met would only put up with ripples of dissatisfaction from the public at the lack of arrests for so long.

Press statements had been done in addition to a witness appeal on all the various social media platforms. Despite the want for information nothing concrete had come forth. A witness appeal board placed at the scene had produced a few calls, but most were crank ones and not great at that. The incident room also had a dedicated hotline. As far as she was concerned, without going into every minutiae of what she was doing or thinking, she had her bases covered, thank you very much.

They were under Archway Bridge and approaching the roundabout with Holloway Road when her phone rang.

'Nash,' she shouted into the speaker in order to be heard over the noise from the convoy.

'Boss, it's Simon from the OP. Our suspect's in the address now. He just arrived carrying what looked like a yoga mat bag. He doesn't appear like the type who'd partake in a stretch and chant session. It's big enough to carry drugs, that's for sure, and he may have the knife in there or on his person,' came back the response from the observation point. A message she and Moretti were overjoyed to hear.

'Maintain your position and great work. We'll be straight to the venue and strike.' Nash completed the call and turned to Moretti.

'Change of plan as you've just gathered. We're going straight to the target address. Our suspect has returned carrying a bag that may contain all we need,' she said as her phone rang again.

'Nash.'

'Pip, it's your reliable and most handsome source handler here. The package has arrived. It's good to go if you are,' said the Silverfox.

'Leave it with me; I'll contact you if I need anything else or if I need to tell you how much it's going to cost you in drinks,' she said as the handler laughed at the other end. To Nash, from all the background noise it sounded like he was in a pub. Lucky for some, she thought as she killed the line.

Nash placed a call to the tactical advisor for the firearms team. She listened and Nash handed over control to her. It was now a wait and see as the team leader relayed the message via personal radio: 'All units from Silver Control, I have the lead from here. Silent approach, direct to target premises, and await further instruction as we run, out.'

The other units acknowledged her last transmission. What was a cacophony of sound changed to lights only as they made their final approach.

It was now 23:00 and the lead cars crawled down the street which was reasonably quiet save for a few people out dealing on a corner and a drunk who was using a hedge as a bed. The mosque's lights were on and the bunches of flowers Nash had seen from the balcony had multiplied in number.

Nash was thankful of the calmness on the street when they arrived as it was about to erupt.

The armed officers silently got out of their cars, leaving the doors open to avoid any noise, and several officers used them as additional cover while they kept an alert pair of eyes out for trouble to the officers who stepped towards the address. The firearms unit had brought their own rapid entry team as Nash's man in the OP had reported it was a reinforced metal door to the house. Nash knew this as she'd contacted a mate on a response team who'd driven past the address, seen the door and relayed the message to her.

Nash and Moretti watched from their car with the windows open. The entry team were waved forward by an armed officer. Two of them carried a set of door spreaders and a compressor. The spreaders were placed in position and activated. This was the part she always loved. The whir of the spreader's mechanism kicked in. As it worked, the wooden frame of the main door attempted in vain to resist the force, finally splintering in surrender.

The entry team stood aside as the metal door wobbled. The lead firearms officer shifted his shoulders and feet in preparation for the entry. The door finally gave way and collapsed inwards with a huge crash as a face appeared and opened an upstairs window.

The calm of the street was lost to shouts of 'Armed police,' continually being barked like a mantra. A contingent of officers brandishing assault weapons and ballistic shields stormed the house. A searchlight, angled from the roof of an Armed Response Vehicle, illuminated the upstairs window causing the person who'd appeared there to shield his eyes.

Nash could hear the commotion as they sat in the car waiting for the all-clear. The man was refusing to cooperate with the officer's instructions. A repeated shout of 'Taser, Taser,' was heard before he froze and dropped from their view thanks to fifty thousand volts of electricity searing through his bare skin.

'It never gets tiring watching this lot in action,' Nash said as Moretti's face showed the same feeling of contentment mixed with euphoria. The topless man they'd seen at the upstairs window was now outside shouting for revenge.

Sandwiched between two armed cops, his hands were bound behind him in plasticuffs. Nash was pleased to see an effort to secure any gunshot residue that may be on his hands had been made by securing his wrists in clear plastic bags. Not that it was any concern of her murder investigation but a live gun would be a result. Snaked metal wires hung from his chest where the prongs from the Taser had penetrated. He stopped shouting as the Taser officer issued a further warning that there'd be another dose if he didn't shut up and calm down.

The tactical advisor approached Nash's car.

'We're all done. You can get your team in now. We'll look after matey boy until he calms down properly,' she said.

Nash phoned Drake to inform him the scene was his now. The armed entry team had the containment. Drake had been in his own vehicle while the entry took place and now left the safety of his car.

Local uniform had now arrived because during the thrill of the raid a crowd had begun to emerge from surrounding houses. Deploying crowd control prior to a raid was out of the question as it could alert their target. More people began to exit the mosque as a result of all the noise. Nash could sense an atmosphere that wasn't conducive to the calm search she was trying to achieve. As she dissected the crowd, she saw the imam approach their car. He came to the driver side where Nash sat with the window still open.

'DI Nash? Is it you? Have you arrested someone for the murder? Is it him? The man over there?' The imam nodded towards the suspect, but Nash made a point of not looking, her senses telling her this could go all wrong, as a small crowd of worshippers had gathered near her car.

Nash decided on a direct approach. She took her five-foot-six frame out of the car and leaned on her door. She was conscious of avoiding conflict should the crowd get hostile.

'Look, we don't know yet. What I'd appreciate is if we could have some space to work?' Nash said to the imam who was only interested in the suspect in the distance.

'So, it could be him, eh? He has caused us nothing but grief with his racist and anti-religious talk and threats of violence,' the voice of an onlooker shouted out from behind the imam.

Fuck, Nash thought as the crowd grew and more uniform officers arrived, including a carrier from the Territorial Support Group who was on the Commissioner's Reserve in case of public disorder. Nash leant towards the imam.

'Please control your congregation, sir. For the sake of the victim and his family's dignity. I will let you know if there's anything found that could link to his death. Otherwise I won't be responsible for how others here react,' she said, nodding towards the yellow jackets arriving by the vanload.

The imam looked at Nash and then over at the TSG carrier. He turned to the crowd and appealed for calm. They made representations, some shouted in the suspect's direction, but they adhered to the imam's request, much to the relief of Moretti and Nash. Uniform officers were now in among the crowd, politely asking them to leave the area. Some listened, others didn't.

Nash joined DI Drake inside the property as the suspect was taken back into the house. Once inside, two armed officers were stationed at the opening while arrangements were put in place for an emergency board-up. No one wanted to be there for longer than required.

The couch was searched by Drake's team and, once deemed clear of any weapons, needles, or evidence, the suspect was told to sit down. Lee Brown was the only person at the address, as they'd hoped. He remained passive but defiant. He knew the consequences should he react again. The metal wires attached to his chest provided a stark reminder. In Brown's head, all the actions the police had taken bolstered his reputation as a dangerous and violent thug. A straightforward knock on the door meant you were a low risk to any officer but when armed cops stormed your property, it meant you were too risky to send in regular plod. The heavier handed the police were, the greater your reputation as a bad boy was on the street. The worse your reputation the greater respect you had from those in the criminal world. Such was the law of the street.

Nash heard a radio request for the search dog and handler who'd been waiting outside to come into the house. As this was made, Brown's body twitched as he cricked his neck from side to side. His torso rippled as he moved. The sound of an excited dog was heard over the radio. Nash's eyes lit up at the news. Brown looked at the floor. He'd been here before and knew that with the arrival of the dog, his time as a free man was limited. As much as a dog bite will hurt, the mutt's nose can inflict greater pain in terms of a custodial sentence when it sniffs out guns and drugs.

'So, are you going to tell me where the gear is or wait for the pooch to rip up half the house? I'm easy but I can't say the same for Samson the dog. He sounds, how would you say, fucking manic,' DI Drake said to Brown who barely looked up.

'Bring it on. There's nothing to be found here. You lot can waste as much fucking time as you like. I've got all evening and then some. In my head, I'm already planning a meeting with my brief for unlawful detention and search,' Brown said, not cracking a smile.

'Well, be sure to give them this,' Drake said as he dropped a copy of the search warrant into Brown's lap, Brown showing his contempt by blowing it to the floor.

A DC approached Drake; a slight male, with a shaved head and weasely-looking eyes.

'You need to come and see this,' he said motioning to Drake. Nash and Moretti followed them through to a back room leaving Brown with two other officers.

The room was lit by a single thirty-watt bulb hung on a ceiling pendant that looked to have been wired in by a trainee sparky. Newspaper cuttings of right-wing demos were plastered on the wall. A selection of bayonets and hunting knives inhabited a shelf alongside Nazi memorabilia. It looked like a shrine to the inhumane.

'None of it's illegal,' Brown shouted from the living room.

'Make sure this is all photographed,' Nash told the DC.

From the kitchen came a shout from the dog handler, 'I need a DC and the suspect. The dog's indicating a find.'

'Fuck.' The only word out of Brown's dry mouth.

The dog handler gently coerced his dog back from the cooker as a DC wearing gloves waited for Brown to be brought closer to the kitchen door to get a good view at what the dog had found.

Once Brown was in sight, the DC opened the oven to reveal a bag. As the DC brought it out from its hiding place, a definite sag to the bottom of the canvas was evident.

Brown looked away as the officer presented his find. The spaniel sat smiling. Tongue hanging out. Eyes wide that shimmered like the still surface of a Loch after fresh rain. The DC with the bag gave Brown the caution the law required in these circumstances prior to asking him any questions.

'Is this your bag?' the DC asked Brown.

Brown didn't reply. Didn't even look at the bag, just continued to stare at the dog with contempt. Contempt for the dog's nose, as well as contempt at himself for being lazy and hiding the bag in a dumb place. All he'd wanted when he got home was to get wasted.

As the DC opened the bag it revealed two kilo blocks of cocaine and a hunting knife with an indented top edge with spiked protrusions like shark teeth and a blade that had an edge that appeared as though it had just been forged. The handle was bound in masking tape. There'd been no attempt at trying to disguise the contents.

'Is this yours?' DI Drake asked Brown who remained staring at the dog, saying nothing.

'I would have thought this oven-ready recipe was a guarded secret. Let's hope the recipe is the right one.' Drake laughed at his own joke as he nodded at the weasel-faced DC.

'OK, let's play it your way. You're nicked for possession with intent to supply. Same caution applies that was given earlier, if you don't understand, I'll repeat it but, going by your silence, I reckon you understood the whole thing. Now, what else are we likely to find?'

There was a brief silence before Brown looked up. 'Rip the place apart if that'll make your Christmas. Now, if you don't mind, I've had enough of this party so I'd like to go to a station, get the fucking metal prongs taken out of my tits, and get a good night's kip,' Brown said sarcastically.

Drake nodded at the armed cops who took Brown out to the waiting van.

'Rip the place apart and seize all the knives,' Nash informed Drake.

'It'll be my pleasure,' he replied enthusiastically.

CHAPTER ELEVEN

It was 3 a.m. when Nash returned Moretti to the marina. The rest of the search had gone as expected. Drugs paraphernalia along with two kilos of cocaine, some reseal bags, and scales were found in a concealed space behind a kitchen unit. Five hundred in cash was also in the bag with the drugs and knife. Nash had requested the knife in the bag be prioritised for forensic examination and DI Drake assured her it would be done.

A decent result but still nothing to link Brown to the murder and she hoped forensics would be able to match blood on the blade of the knife with the victim's. Drake had seized all the knives he could and Nash was confident they'd maximised the source information.

Where the five hundred came into play was too early to say. Hussein hadn't been robbed. Drake's team would be conducting interviews later today once Brown had a rest period. Nash was happy for Drake's team to crack on as she had nothing to question Brown about just yet and didn't want to start his custody clock ticking for her murder. Let Drake use up his own custody time dealing with Brown, giving the lab time to work up the knife, and hopefully returning with the result Nash needed.

'Coffee? Or do you need to get away quickly?' Moretti asked as he unclipped his seat belt and leant back in between the centre console for his coat and the man-bag he'd thrown on the back seat. Nash always had the car's heater on full and it felt like a sauna.

'I'm still wide awake so a coffee will do me no harm. You redeemed yourself today, Nick,' she replied.

They walked towards his barge and took in the crisp night air. The sky above glittered with stars. More could've been viewed if it wasn't for the houses and street lights as well as exhaust fumes. Moretti unlocked the barge door and they stepped inside. Sensor lights were triggered that illuminated a kitchen-cum-living area.

'Take a seat. Milk no sugar, right?' Moretti asked.

'Right,' she replied.

'I never knew you had a penchant for painting, you dark horse?' Nash said, much to Moretti's confusion.

'I don't...' Moretti turned and saw what Nash had referred to. An artist's easel had been erected at the end of the living room. As quick as the recognition transpired, they heard footsteps.

Moretti turned back to where the sound of light footsteps on the wooden floor emanated. Tabatha emerged dressed in a long white T-shirt that Moretti recognised as his from the image of The Ramones that adorned the front. Her blonde hair defined her elfin face coupled with a ruffled just-got-out-of-bed look that accented her deep blue eyes that struggled with the lamplight. Moretti realised he was staring and averted his gaze.

'Well, do I get introduced?' Nash jostled Moretti who ran his fingers through his hair while he glanced back at Tabatha.

'Sure. Tabatha, DI Nash, Pip, I mean, this is Tabatha,' he stumbled through the introductions.

'Hi,' Tabatha said quietly and with an awkward wave of her hand as she walked towards Moretti.

'Sorry about the painting, I'll move it later today. I heard voices so came out to make sure it was you and no one else,' Tabatha said as she smiled coyly and adjusted her T-shirt making sure it sat dutifully above her knees and wasn't rucked up at the back.

'I've no issue with it; you can leave it where it is. Can't wait to see the finished picture,' Moretti said, hoping he sounded genuine as he meant it.

Tabatha returned his smile, nodded at Nash, and left to go back to the spare room. The fabric from Moretti's T-shirt embraced her naked butt cheeks as she exited. He noticed how it looked way better on her than him. He also wondered where he'd left it and remembered it was in the utility room, clean and folded so easy to find without turning out his drawers.

'Well, things have certainly changed here, Nick, you sly—'

'Whoa! Tabatha doesn't live here, well not in the way you're implying, she's staying here while her boat's heating gets repaired,' Moretti said as he handed Nash her coffee.

'Must be nice having an artist on-board, skipper?' Nash said as she stifled a laugh.

'Very funny. As it goes, it would be the other way around.' Moretti immediately regretted his response but realised it was too late to retract it.

'Huh? Don't tell me you can paint too? This evening just gets better and better!'

'No. I can't and don't paint.'

'So? If you don't paint, then why would she be getting her kit off? Oh, fuck me, Nick, she's not a bloody tom?' Nash said putting her cup down.

'Keep your voice down!' Moretti exclaimed as he looked towards the door Tabatha had left through.

Nash held her mouth as tears of laughter started forming and her shoulders moved uncontrollably. She drew her legs up to her chest and leant her head over the sofa's back. Moretti decided to let her know the rest.

'She's not a prostitute, she's a dancer,' he said.

'Oh! What? Ballet? Tango? Ballroom?' Nash mocked as she leaned in closer to Moretti.

'None. She's a dancer in a club,' he said.

Nash looked at Moretti.

'Did I hear right? She's a pole dancer? Nick, you're telling me you have a pole dancer living on your boat?'

'No, no, I'm not telling you that at all… well, she's a stripper, I don't know about the pole thing but I suppose she could use that as a prop, so yeah, that's exactly what I'm telling you and you only. Pip, there's more to a person than their job. Take a look at what's on the easel, that's where her true talent lies.' Moretti indicated the painting with his mug, the picture showed the promise of the boats lined up on the marina. A rough black outline already began to reveal what the picture would look like once completed.

Nash's laughter settled as she dabbed her eyes with her sleeve and picked her mug back up.

'So, you've seen her at work then, if you know that's where her talents lie?'

'Nope. She's a neighbour. I only know her as a neighbour. The most I've seen of her is when our paths have crossed between shifts and the odd get-together at a community party – and just now.' He got up and went back to the kitchen and made himself another coffee.

'I think I'll skip another, Nick. I'm more tired than I thought, and it's been quite a revealing day,' Nash said as she craned her neck.

'Suit yourself. I'll see you tomorrow at eight. I will be on time, promise. I'll get the train,' Moretti replied.

'Are you sure, Detective Sergeant? Don't you fancy another lie-in?'

With that, Moretti's face flushed as he ushered Nash to the door. She still carried her half-filled mug.

'Keep the coffee; just bring the mug back, clean,' he told her as she left the boat smiling and trying not to laugh out loud at Moretti's awkwardness.

As she heard the door close, Nash took a drink, and started walking back to her car. As she approached the door, she threw the coffee to the ground.

He never could make a decent cup of coffee, she thought.

* * *

The trains were delayed due to frost on the line and Moretti prayed that one would come soon as he was sick of standing on a platform packed full of irate commuters. Moretti instinctively patted his pocket and felt the reassuring outline of his warrant card that doubled up as his annual travel ticket for up to seventy miles outside of London. As he waited, his phone vibrated. It was a text from the DS on DI Drake's team. They'd be interviewing Brown all morning and would update Nash on anything significant. He didn't bother responding. The DS would receive a message showing it had been delivered and read.

An announcement came over the speaker that the trains were cancelled. A low groan went up from the platform as people made their way back to the stairs. Moretti got another text as he emerged from the station.

Turn right at the top.

He did so and there was Nash sat in the job car.

'How did you know?' Moretti asked as he got in glad at the sight of her.

'Female intuition. That and the radio announced the trains were all screwed, so I figured that after only a few hours' sleep, I'd drop by and save your arse from walking,' she responded pleased with herself.

'Well thank God for female intuition,' Moretti said as he clapped his gloved hands together to get warmed up.

'So where to now?' Moretti asked.

'I can't sit around while the fella from last night's banged up. Let's pay Mr Hussein's widow a visit. See how the land lies after last night. The FLO contacted me this morning and said she'd been cooperating so far, and hadn't deviated from the account she'd had to repeat. Husband was out playing cards as he did every week at the same time, same place, and that he was sliced open – not her words – when he nearly got home. There's got to be more to this. We must be missing something,' she said.

'Should we get a forensic behavioural psychologist?' Moretti said.

'Very funny. Remember the last time the DCI came up with that bright idea? Had us running around on a profile that fit most of the coppers on the team. Well, the men anyway. I had money on you in the office sweep, Nick.' Nash winked as Moretti held his mouth agape.

'I'm not a bloke with an average state education, living at home with one, possibly two parents, and a tendency towards violence but only when provoked,' he replied as they set off.

'Absolutely. You're a bloke with a degree in unpredictability and a doctorate for dropping yourself in the shit.' She smiled.

The drive went smoothly, and they soon found themselves back at St Thomas's Road. A police van was parked up and two uniformed officers in high-visibility jackets were out on foot as part of a community reassurance patrol initiated by the commander for the Borough.

'I see the witness appeal board's still up and not defaced. Let's hope it stays that way,' Nash said as she stopped outside the victim's address.

Nash fastened her new coat by the belt as the wind picked up, throwing a discarded witness appeal flyer into the air that became embedded in a hedge that bordered the Husseins' small patch of soil that qualified as a garden. The gate that opened onto a pathway towards the house hung loose while a child's trike and pram acted as ornamental garden features. From the green mould on the plastic they looked to have been there for some time. A rare thing for any child's toy to remain outside in the same place without being nicked. To a drug addict desperate for the next fix, they'd have made an easy sell to the right person.

They approached the door and Moretti pressed the buzzer. They could hear the sound of a chime from inside. After a short while an outline of a figure appeared at the frosted glass that ran down the central part of the door.

'Yes? Who is it?' a female's voice asked. Her English sounded strained despite the full reply.

'Hi, it's DI Nash from the police, can I come in please?'

The door opened slightly, and Nash's eyes were drawn down to a boy of no more than five stood at the base of an adult female's legs.

'You aren't who my mum speaks to, so why are you here?' he asked with the confidence of a kid raised in London and a boy who'd elevated himself to head of his household through circumstances he couldn't comprehend.

Nash shifted her feet, desperate to get inside and out of the cold but the pocket sentry had other ideas.

'I'm from the same team as the officer your mum speaks to; I'm her boss, not your mum's, obviously, the officer's. Is your mum in, we'd like to see her?' Nash asked again with a smile.

The boy looked down the hallway then turned back to Nash.

'She's sleeping. You have to go away now, come back later,' he said with a jolt of his head to emphasise his conviction.

'Who's looking after you? Who's this lady?' Nash asked motioning to the mute woman who'd opened the door.

'This is my aunty, she can't speak very good English,' he said.

Just as the boy started to shut the door a new voice spoke.

'Who is it?' they demanded in English.

Before Nash could reply, the boy answered in Urdu. As he finished the victim's wife appeared, opened the door fully, apologised, and let them in.

Nash and Moretti removed their shoes and placed them on a mat by the door along with the others. A mixture of children's and women's footwear but also an adult male's. Outside and indoor pairs. One pair of each lined up neatly.

The young boy ran upstairs, and his aunty followed chatting in Urdu on the way up.

'Please come through and have a seat. I will make tea, yes?' Mrs Hussein said.

'That would be lovely, thanks. Both with milk no sugar,' Nash replied with a warm tone.

A two-bar electric fire warmed the living room they were in. A Christmas tree was up along with other decorations. Pictures of the family adorned the walls and occupied much of the spare space. Moretti picked up one of the pictures sat atop a wooden mantelpiece. It showed the victim along with his wife and child. A professional shot that appeared to have been taken on holiday judging by the clear blue sky and white sand.

'That was taken on our last holiday to Dubai,' Mrs Hussein said when she entered the room and put down a tray of mugs and a plate of biscuits.

Moretti placed the picture back where he'd found it and sat down.

'So, tell me. You arrested the man from two doors down last night? I knew it was him who murdered my husband. It just had to be him. He never had a decent word to say about anyone from my community,' she said as she poured the hot, light-brown tea from a metal pot.

'I'm afraid the person in question was arrested on matters unconnected to your husband's murder. We happened to be in the area as a result of our investigation,' Nash was quick to reply, quashing any hope she may have harboured that the investigation was complete.

'But the imam said he spoke with you and you would tell him of any developments with the man arrested?' she fired back.

'That's correct. If, and it's a big if, he had any connection with this investigation I would be telling you. I'm sorry the news isn't what you want to hear,' Nash explained.

She always made a point of giving any bad news directly and not letting the victim's family dwell on rumour and street gossip. That kind of talk had a way of exploding out of all proportion and it was the last thing she wanted or needed right now. She leant forward to pick up her mug and started with questions she needed answers to.

'Was your husband out of the house a lot?'

'What do you mean?'

'Well, did you always know where he was?'

'Of course I knew where he was. He is… was, my husband. We had no secrets.' Her eyes held Nash's.

'So, you always knew where he was and who he was with?'

'Of course not… not all the time. What wife does, Inspector? Does your husband know where you are every hour of the day?'

'I'm not married,' she replied.

'So how can you question my marriage when you know so little of marriage yourself?'

'It's my job to ask questions, Mrs Hussein, that's why.'

'But he would always tell me when he got home.'

'Did your husband work?'

'Yes, he worked. We couldn't afford to go on holiday to Dubai if he didn't. He was an accountant. He looked after the mosque's accounts along with other private ones, too. He was a trustee at the mosque. A very honourable and trustworthy man,' she said before sipping her tea, clearly annoyed and riled by Nash's questions.

'I don't doubt that he was anything but trustworthy and honest. Did he ever speak of any enemies or people he'd fallen out with recently who'd want to–'

'Kill him? No. Enemies? Yes, of course. You try being a Muslim living in London and not have enemies. They are everywhere we walk, casting eyes of disgust and hatred at us, calling us names, degrading us through hate speech, but I can't think of anyone in particular, no.'

'Do you have any thoughts as to why anyone would want to kill your husband? I appreciate it's a difficult question, but I must explore as much as I can,' Nash asked.

'No. I have no idea and the notion that someone would want to… to… murder him in such a cold-blooded way is…' She began to sob.

Nash handed her a tissue from a near-empty box on the small table where their mugs were placed. She knew the widow had had enough. Nash sipped her now tepid tea and mulled over whether she needed to push her any more at this point and decided she didn't. All the research being conducted was only corroborating what she was telling her: her husband had been a pillar of the community whose only vice was a backroom card school that harmed no one.

'Mrs Hussein, I appreciate your time. I can't imagine what you must be going through at the moment. Thank you for your hospitality. I will leave you in peace while you deal with the funeral arrangements. I appreciate all the space you've given me to explore the circumstances of your husband's death in more detail with the pathologist. There may be more questions as the enquiry progresses but for today, we'll bid you farewell. I'll be in touch as soon as I establish anything you need to know. In the meantime, DC Lewis will continue to support you as your Family Liaison Officer. I tried to get an FLO of your faith but I'm afraid there was no one available. I will keep trying if that would be of help?' Nash said.

Mrs Hussein shook her head. Nash nodded at Moretti and they got up to go. Mrs Hussein got up and pressed her hands down her niqab and escorted them to the door. They put on their shoes and with a final goodbye they left.

The car was where they'd left it, and all looked to be as it should. Nash did a once over before she got in. Checking all four wheels were still in place and there was no damage.

'What do you make of her?' Moretti asked Nash as she pulled away.

'She's a woman grieving the tragic and sudden loss of a man she adored. She has absolutely no idea why her husband's been murdered, and a desperate need to have him buried as soon as possible. That's my impression,' Nash replied, resolutely.

'I'm not heartless, Pip. Let's hope Drake comes up with something from Brown or forensics come back with a match,' he said as he stared out the window.

Nash had listened but was deep in thought as she drove. 'Get the FLO to request an examination of his computer. I'm happy for the tech guys to image his hard drive rather than remove the whole thing. Let's take a look at what he's been up to, or not, online: social media, chat rooms, Internet search history, anything that might give us a clue to something he hasn't been sharing with his wife,' she asked Moretti as he made notes in his blue book.

There'd been a directive about not routinely seizing computers in every murder investigation as the storage facilities were at capacity and technical labs were so understaffed, they couldn't service what they had. Much of what was seized ended up as more of a fishing expedition than evidential retrieval. Child protection investigations took priority, and in other investigations, a clear reason was needed before forensic IT work would be considered. Nash was now able to show a need for Jared's PC to be examined and a reason why it was needed.

'Sure, I'll see to it,' Moretti said as Nash's phone rang, and she answered it in her usual way.

'Nash.'

'DI Pippa Nash, MIT 2?' a voice asked.

'Yes, who's this?'

'Diane Fullerton from forensic services regarding your urgent submission?'

'Go on,' she said with a spark of hope.

'I'm afraid there's nothing coming back from the knife that could link to your victim. There's no trace of blood at all on the blade. I have also compared the cutting edge with the samples taken by Dr King and under the microscope they show a clean cut whereas this blade, although never used, hasn't a smooth cutting edge. Quite common for steel to be like this when examined closely.

'In fact the blade's brand new by all appearances. Never been used. I have lifted some prints and DNA from skin on the masking-taped handle that comes back to Lee Brown, the person in custody. I've e-mailed you a full report, but I spoke with a DI Drake who requested you be informed immediately?' the technician said.

'That's very good of you, thank you.' Nash terminated the call.

'I heard that. What now?' Moretti asked as she paused at a set of lights.

'We're off to Islington nick for a chat with Lee Brown,' Nash responded as she stared out of the car's windscreen at the line of traffic ahead.

'But there's no match? Why are we wasting time with him?' Moretti asked, confused at Nash's train of thought.

'Have you got any better ideas? Call it gut instinct but he's the only person in custody who has access to the type of weapon our killer likes, and he may know more than he's letting on.'

CHAPTER TWELVE

The back yard at Islington police station was littered with police vehicles. A van unit were busy unloading a compliant prisoner from the rear cage and they followed them into the custody reception area.

The low glow of fluorescent lights greeted them along with the stale stench of sweat and spent meals that awaited disposal on a metal serving trolley. The booking-in area was up ahead on a raised platform. A burly-looking custody sergeant occupied a raised chair that gave him a domineering and judicial view of his domain. He glanced up in their direction and paid them no attention – a Pavlovian response whenever the prisoner entry door opened and closed.

Moretti moved forward.

'Stop where you are,' came the stentorian voice of the custody sergeant. Moretti looked around then realised it was aimed at him.

'Where's your prisoner?' the custody officer asked him, not looking up from his typing as the person he was managing had his pockets turned out and the contents displayed on the counter.

Moretti knew what was coming. The custody officer was sat atop a tall swivel chair high enough for his feet to remain off the floor despite his standing height that Moretti witnessed as he slid off the stool to retrieve a property sheet printed from the machine behind him.

'I know, I know. I shouldn't have come through the door for prisoner entry only. I apologise but it was the quickest route in,' Moretti offered up in mitigation. A mitigation which was, he realised straightaway, weak and misguided.

'I'll let you off on this occasion. Your DI had the decency to call ahead and say you'd be over to speak with chummy in cell fifteen. He's been charged and remanded in custody so when I've finished with this one I'll have him brought out and see if he wants to talk to you,' the custody sergeant stated as he peered into the computer monitor's screen and tapped away at the keyboard with each index finger.

The sergeant finished up what he was doing, and the arresting officer took his detainee down to his lodgings. Nash and Moretti had been waiting in an area known as the goldfish bowl where a board showed who was currently staying.

It was quiet; only fifteen out of the twenty-six cells were in use. As the sergeant entered the goldfish bowl, he shut the door and sat down. His eyes red and sore with tiredness from working under weak strip lighting for too long.

'OK, your man is all charged, in custody, and waiting for court in the morning. I'd prefer it if you told him he was going for a cigarette break rather than interview while you're in the cell passage as others may hear and if he ends up in prison, word could get back he's grassed. I have his safety to consider while he's on my watch,' he stated.

Nash nodded her approval at the sergeant's request.

'Fine by me,' Moretti replied.

'Good. I took the liberty of letting the custody inspector know. He's had him out and he's happy to see you without his solicitor. If that changes, then you stop the interview and bring him back to me, agreed?' the sergeant said, leaning forward, looking at Nash and Moretti with his hands out in front, palms facing each other.

'Agreed,' Nash said.

Moretti signed Lee Brown out for interview, while Nash went with the gaoler to get him from his cell. As she strolled down the corridor, she could hear low moans coming from a cell, crying from another, and at the far end, a rhythmic banging shook a door as someone kicked away from inside the cell like a disgruntled horse in a stable. It would be hurting as their shoes had been removed and placed on the floor outside. Nash took the keys from the gaoler, dropped the metal cell wicket, and observed Brown sat on his economy blue mattress. Satisfied it was safe, Nash opened the door.

A psychological message was being sent to Brown that Nash was his saviour coming to get him out. The idea being that Nash hadn't locked him up but was able to let him out. At least, that's what her interview training had advised her. Brown had other ideas.

'About fuckin' time. I need a cup of tea and something to eat. I'm starvin', darlin',' he said as he picked up a Styrofoam cup and handed it to Nash.

Nash took it and gave it to the gaoler.

'Am I wearing an apron with "Chef" written on it?' Nash said as she turned to the gaoler. 'Make it three teas when you can, please,' she asked as the gaoler took the cup and muttered under her breath as she did.

Nash escorted Brown along the corridor to the interview room. Brown moved slowly in front with a street swagger and a fuck-you attitude. They entered the interview room, where Brown was instructed to sit with his back to the soundproofed wall. Moretti and Nash occupied the seats closest to the door. Moretti flicked the switch that indicated the room was now in use and activated the recording. There was a knock and the gaoler interrupted bringing in the teas and exited quickly. Nash ripped open a small sachet of sugar and pushed two over towards Brown who eyed her suspiciously as he tore the top off one with his teeth and poured the contents in before dropping the empty packet on the floor. Brown stuck his index finger in the hot liquid and with his eyes firmly fixed on Nash, stirred it twice before he removed his finger and sucked off the residue. He leant back in his seat and put his arms behind his head.

Moretti looked at Nash who gave a nod and they began.

'This is an intelligence interview with…? Please state your full name,' Nash said.

'Lee Brown.'

'The date and time's recorded by the machine. We're in the interview room at Islington police station. I'm DI Nash and the other officer present is…?'

'DS Moretti.'

'We're both attached to the Homicide and Serious Crime Command,' Nash continued.

'Very pleased for you both. Now, as I told the uniform inspector earlier, there's nothing I can help you with, absolutely fuck all. I needed a leg stretch though and any time out of that cell suits me. Nice tea by the way,' Brown said as he raised his cup to the video camera that wasn't being used.

'You still agree to have this interview without your solicitor?'

'Yep.'

'If you change your mind at any time during the interview, let me know and we'll arrange one for you in person or by phone. I'm saying all this but as far as I'm concerned this is an intelligence interview only and I won't be asking any questions about the offences for which you've been charged and remanded in police custody, I just want to make that perfectly clear. Do you understand?'

'Crack on, Inspector, I'm going nowhere for the time being as it's quite a bit warmer in here than it is down the hall.' Brown continued to lean back. A grin spread across his face that revealed a gold rear tooth.

'OK. Knives,' Nash said.

'What about them? I've a cutlery drawer full of 'em. At least I did until that twat with the surname of a duck took them all,' he finished as he looked up at the ceiling, his mind drawn to DI Drake.

'You would appear to be a man who may know quite a bit more about knives, where they can be obtained, and that's something I'd be interested in,' Nash said.

'Really? Try Argos, they do loads of 'em. I know you said you weren't no chef but you've cooked up enough charges already and left me on simmer.' He shook his head and tapped the desk.

'I want to find the knife that was used to kill Mr Hussein, what's wrong with that?' Nash said.

Brown ignored the question and continued with his diatribe of derision.

'Anyhow you should know where to get decent blades being a woman. All that time spent cookin' for your fellas. How many you got lined up, eh? Pretty thing like you won't be able to keep them away, I bet. Is that why you're so interested? Need one for protection now?' Brown said as he laughed and tipped his chair back.

'You're quite the comedian aren't you, Lee?' Nash said as she kept her eyes on his.

'I'm on all week, love,' he said as he bent forwards and leaned on the desk, staring at the recorder. He paused for a moment and they let him. He sat back and rubbed his eyes then spoke.

'The other fella, copper, at my house mentioned something about that Muslim who was slaughtered like a lamb the other night. Well, it weren't me and it weren't any knife I had neither,' Brown replied.

'I'm not asking you about that. I'm asking if you've heard anything about a rare knife, a unique knife that you don't see much in places like Argos or hunting magazines? They may have talked of buying or selling a very sharp blade. The kind you'd love,' Nash said.

Nash watched Brown who remained poised, now balanced using the rear legs of the chair and the wall for support.

'So, you want me as a grass, is that it?' Brown grunted at them.

'What I want is to find the person who killed a decent man in a London street, and we figured a man with your knowledge of criminality and weaponry may know some more about who has access to decent quality knives other than you. Call it a community service,' Nash retorted.

Brown dropped his torso forward and leaned on the table. Moretti and Nash remained as they were.

'Community? What fuckin' community would that be then? One where if you're not black or Muslim you don't fit in, that community? Fuck 'em, I say. I ain't got time for them, and I ain't servin' time for 'em neither.'

Nash shifted in her chair. Her anger began to rise at the person in front of her. She concentrated on her breath the way she'd been trained by her teacher in Tottenham while in his dojo and the feelings subsided. Moretti noticed the change in her and intervened.

'Look, you can say what you like but you live there, and we have a duty to take knives off the street. I think you can help and by doing that, help yourself too. You're looking at a decent stretch inside, Lee. Possession with intent to supply won't go down well with any judge. Not now there's a huge pressure on the system to keep people like you banged up and off the streets. So why don't you do yourself a favour and think about how you could help yourself by helping us?' Moretti said.

Brown looked at Nash. His eyes blanked, mouth still. A vein in his temple pulsated.

'Why should I help the filth? What have you lot ever done for me other than fuck me about on a daily basis, for no reason, I might add?'

Nash leaned towards Brown. Both locked eyes and remained impassive. Nash was the first to intentionally break the silence.

'I'll level with you. I don't care if you rot in a prison cell with an entire wing waiting to draw straws to grab your virginity. I hope you get the maximum amount of years, but I have a murder I intend to solve and I'm here to ask for your help with that.' Nash came across as antagonistic, which she was trying to be.

Brown's face began to crease as the vein beat and became more pronounced than before. Nash knew she'd hit the spot and continued with the pressure.

'I'm a reasonable person. I'm prepared to write a letter to the judge saying how you helped combat knife crime and reduce violence. Better if you give up who has the weapon that happened to be used to kill my victim. If it's a no from you, then who knows what fate awaits you. So, what do you say?'

Brown leapt across the table as soon as Nash had finished. The chair he was sat in flew back into the wall with enough force to cause an indentation in the plasterboard. Nash had a hunch she'd get that reaction and as Brown grabbed both her lapels Moretti wrestled him to the table. Nash bashed the emergency strip that ran along the back wall behind them and an alarm activated outside in the block. The interview room door burst open and Brown was unceremoniously dragged back to his cell by a troop of uniform officers. Moretti turned off the recorder and adjusted his tie.

'Great work, Pip. Just great!' Moretti exclaimed as he shook his head and lifted his man-bag from the chair he'd placed it on.

'I was reasonable, he chose to overreact. Let him stew on it for a bit then we'll see how he is,' Nash said as she took her coat and left the interview room.

The custody sergeant approached Nash as she came out of the room and back around to the main custody area.

'I'll leave you to write up his record as to what took place and I'll have the CD copy of the interview too,' the sergeant said.

Nash took the clipboard that had Brown's record attached and moved to the goldfish bowl to write up her account of why Brown was removed. Moretti found the metal cupboard that contained the cups of grit that passed for prisoners' coffee and made himself and the custody sergeant a drink. Nash could make her own as far as he was concerned.

CHAPTER THIRTEEN

Nash got up to tip the dregs of tea into a trailing geranium she'd positioned on the windowsill of her office. A plant she recognised as being much like her. It required the minimum of care and fuss and if left to her own devices would develop and grow in the direction it intended. She looked out over the parade square now full of cars and wondered how she was going to make any headway with the enquiry.

All they had so far was: the victim's identity and confirmation he was murdered by a knife with a distinctively sharp, surgical, cutting edge that wasn't a scalpel. The cut was too long to be caused by a razor blade and too clean to have been caused by any sort of wire. There were a number of knives that fit the description and it was proving problematic to narrow them down to any manufacturer in the UK, let alone abroad. Metal detectors and portable knife arches at tube stations proved a useful deterrent. She'd hoped Brown would know of a blade that was doing the rounds that would be classed as very desirable, sharp and a worthy addition to a collector like him. She was disappointed he'd not come across anything like that. Trace evidence at the scene was limited to the victim, trainer marks, grainy CCTV of the suspect and knife and many others who could have used the footpath and immediate area on a daily basis. If only cats could talk, she'd have interviewed the old woman's in the block where the killer had been.

Nash moved from the window and reclined in her office chair as she sifted through a mountain of new paperwork that had arrived on her desk. She had no filing system to speak of. No *In*, *Out*, or *Pending* tray. Detectives just dumped the completed actions and statements on her desk for her to read in the knowledge that she always did and never missed a trick.

As she mulled over her pending work, her mobile rang.

'Nash,' she answered.

'DI Nash, it's the custody officer at Islington. Mr Brown wishes to talk again.'

'We're on our way,' Nash replied.

The custody area was busier this time and Moretti played the game by using the correct entrance on the ground floor. Another Borough DC told him the combination for the door and he noted it on the palm of his hand. They walked along the corridor and Nash checked through the window before she entered the main custody area. She'd learnt from experience to check before you entered. Last thing she wanted was an inmate escape.

The new custody officer attended the cell with Nash and escorted Brown to the interview room.

'I'll have an officer outside the room just in case. I heard what happened last time,' she said as she left Brown in Nash and Moretti's care.

Brown appeared weary and custody-worn. His eyes were red and puffed up from lack of sleep and his stomach rumbled as he sat. He was dressed in a paper suit as he'd decided to soil his cell and smear excrement over the walls in protest at his incarceration. Nash was thankful Brown had taken the option to shower. Interview legalities over, she began.

'OK, Lee, we're back at your request so what is it you want to tell us?' Nash said as Brown leaned on the desk, head low, and scratched the side of his stubble.

'Before I say anything, right, I want guarantees that I'll get a sentence reduction if I tell you what I've heard,' he said.

'I'll level with you. I'll write a letter telling the judge how your information has helped police. That's all I can do. The rest is up to the judge. I have no control over that,' Nash replied as Brown leaned back and wiped both palms of his hands down his face while looking to the ceiling. Nash knew he would talk. He had no option. If he said nothing, then the custodial term would be what it was. If he gave them something that produced a result for her, it could be reduced.

Brown shifted his powerful neck from side to side and released tension. He placed his forearms on the desk.

'All right, have it your way. First off, I had nothing to do with the fella's murder. I don't like 'em but I'm not a killer. An associate of mine sent a geezer my way. He was looking for a decent knife. The one you lot have. I'd showed this geezer the blade, but he said he'd already made other arrangements. He gave me five hundred notes as a goodwill gesture and to keep my mouth shut. That's it.' Brown leant back and held his arms open as he looked between Nash and Moretti.

'Who is this associate of yours that hooked you up?' Nash asked.

'Nah, no deal. I'm not naming that fella as I'd be dead,' Brown said.

'Then who's the guy you saw? Name, description, telephone number you got him on. Everything you know about him,' Nash said.

'Look, he phoned me off a number that's in my own phone that you lot have. He'd called on the day you nicked me as I'd met him with the weapon and brought it back to my place. I was going to lay it down overnight and move it on. Shit happens.'

'What time did they call?'

'Dunno. It was after midday and I got no other calls after him. The number I gave him was for his use only. He insisted on that as he didn't want the line to be engaged if he made contact. I had no issue with it.'

'What's his name?' Nash pushed again.

Brown wiped his mouth and began rocking in his seat. He pushed his nicotine-stained fingers across his scalp no longer looking at either of them. Moretti shot Nash a side-glance. She remained as she was. No reaction, no pressure on Brown to talk.

'Gary. That's the name he gave me, anyway. I know you're gonna ask so I may as well tell you. He told me to bring the blade over to a flat off St Paul's Road. Top floor 64c,' Brown said with a sigh.

'What colour's the door?' Nash asked him.

'Green.'

'Go on, what happened next?' Moretti continued.

'I get there and buzz the bell and he lets me up. I go in and lay the knife out on a kitchen table. He looks but doesn't touch anything then he tells me it's not what he's after and that he's sorted now but wanted a look-see just in case mine was more his style. He goes out behind a curtain and brings through a pucka-looking hard case.' Brown paused then continued, relieved to offload the burden of knowledge.

'He pops the lock and opens her up. I'm tellin' you it was a thing of beauty he had in there. I've never seen anythin' like it. The blade were dark and polished and the handle was carved out of wood no nonsense. It wasn't for decoration neither. It looked lethal and like it could cut through metal like it was lard. It's no wonder he didn't want mine. I never touched the thing although he offered me to have a hold, which I thought was a fuckin' liberty. Get me dabs all over that. My reckoning is that he took me for a mug. He handed over the bundle of notes, said it was for my time and to keep schtum. I left and went home. The rest's history.'

Brown's shoulders slumped as he slouched back in his seat.

'Describe the fella?' Nash asked.

'I can't. He wore a balaclava with no mouth, hood, and gloves, dark glasses, too. He said it was for his own protection, but it wasn't his knife. He'd bought it for someone else. I didn't believe him as he stroked the fuckin' thing like it was his pet,' Brown said, looking between them for the next question.

'How do you know it was a man other than the name Gary?' Moretti asked.

'He had a bloke's voice and the way he carried himself was like a fella; look, I ain't sayin' any more. You've got enough to go and find him so any chance of a tea now?'

CHAPTER FOURTEEN

Back at Hendon, Nash fed all the new information to the enquiry team and the intelligence cell quickly got to work. They'd retrieved the number Brown said had contacted from his mobile phone while he was still in custody being charged with possession of drugs. The number from the phone was supplied with Brown's consent. At least they'd established an angle to work on. Idle hands weren't something Nash encouraged with her team. If cops had too much time on their hands it generally led to chaos and mouse catching instead of being out doing what they were trained to do: catching criminals and mopping up mess.

Nash heard a knock on her door and Moretti entered. He sat in a comfy chair she had in her office for visitors, bollockings, and comfort to those who needed to talk.

'Anything back from Intel yet?' Moretti asked.

'I've got a couple of officers over at the address Brown gave. They're looking for an observation point so we can cover it. Once that's done, we can decide our next approach. Obviously, if this is our man then we need to react quickly. We may have lost our chance now word will be out Brown has been lifted. We just have to hope our target is confident Brown won't have talked to us,' Nash said.

Moretti nodded in agreement.

'I'm concerned, Pip. We're getting nowhere here and with every hour that passes we're further away from securing anything of forensic value unless we can recover the knife and we can link it to the killer and the victim,' Moretti said.

'Look, why don't we contact the behavioural psychologist again, you know, the one you fancied, Dr Miller, Charlotte Miller? Charlotte the Harlo–'

'We can see her in an hour. I gave her a call for old times' sake and she said pop over and, for God's sake, stop referring to her as a prostitute, will you? What is it you have against your fellow women? First Tabatha, now Charlotte?' Moretti asked.

'Nothing. You do have an eye for a blonde though, you've gotta admit that?'

'Neither confirm nor deny. Now, can we crack on please? We'll take my car and I don't want any crumbs in there,' Moretti said as he produced his car keys from his trouser pocket.

* * *

They pulled up outside the residential house in West Hampstead. Moretti turned off the engine, sat back, and looked at the detached Edwardian property. An imposing double-fronted house with a concrete roof porch supported by circular stone pillars. He knew it was all Charlotte's as a result of a divorce settlement. Her ex was a banker in the city, but she'd described him in more derogatory terms when he'd asked her what he did for employment.

He'd worked with her on a previous enquiry; they'd had dinner one evening in a small boutique restaurant off Hampstead High Street. He'd left her place at six the next morning. He hoped she'd forgiven him but by her voice on the telephone that sounded doubtful.

He rang the bell and a petite woman, mid-forties, with a looked-after body and tied back brunette hair, answered the door.

'Well, well, well. Look what the drains have thrown up. Come in, I'll be back down in a minute. I'm on the phone in my office. Make yourselves at home. Nick will know where everything is.' She turned and skipped up the stairs.

'Fuck me, Nick. You sly, sly dog, you.' Nash whacked him on the arm with her hand.

'We were drunk, it happened once. I thought we'd agreed that would be it. Maybe I got the wrong message,' he said more to himself than Nash.

'You're not that great with us women are you, lover boy?'

'No. No, I'm not, Detective Inspector. Now please get the mugs. They're in the top left cupboard and the coffee's in the container underneath. She has it black, no sugar. I do remember some things and others I won't be discussing with you,' he said.

Nash smiled and found the mugs. Moretti sat on a Tolix stool that tucked under the handmade oak breakfast bar and waited for Charlotte's return. He could hear her melodious voice upstairs and his mind drifted back to when they'd drunkenly made the climb to her bed. He'd enjoyed her company, and the sex, but realised he was too keen on remaining single to enter anything that resembled a relationship. Not that she'd given any indication she was seeking one. He heard the door close and her feet pad towards the stairs. She spoke as she descended.

'OK, I'm all yours, so to speak,' Charlotte said as she joined them.

Nash gave a juvenile smirk and Moretti shot her a look that said "knock it off".

'Thanks. Sorry to gatecrash you but we're in a fix here and could do with some direction,' Moretti explained as Charlotte occupied a stool opposite them both.

She cradled her coffee and awaited further information. Moretti could already feel this was going to be hard work.

'Have you seen the news about the guy who was killed outside the mosque?' Moretti asked her.

'Yes. Couldn't miss it, it's on most news channels putting quite a dampener on the festive spirit if I'm honest,' came Charlotte's curt reply.

Moretti ignored the barb and continued.

'What's your initial take on a possible suspect?'

'Nick, you know I never speculate on the basis of media information alone. You'll have to tell me more, but I will want paying. Work's not as it used to be. I'll give you a discount as it's you,' she responded with a wry smile.

'No win no fee?' Nash added.

Charlotte looked in her direction but said nothing. Moretti intervened.

'That's not in my gift to give but might be in hers,' he said indicating Nash. Nash continued where Moretti had left.

'I'll see what I can do but, in the meantime, how about a steer? Look, I'm not looking to use this evidentially. I could just do with some professional knowledge as to who I need to be looking for. There's not much to go on so you can have what I know.' Nash felt like she was begging but saw this more as a professional barter to another human being who liked to see the right person put away for the crime as much as she did.

'I don't have the budget for your service. I'm trying to track down this person before he or she kills again,' she added.

Charlotte smiled at Nash as she moved from the breakfast bar and brought over the coffee pot and refilled their mugs. Nash saw this as a good sign. Moretti saw it as a blessed welcome as he needed more caffeine.

'Look, I'm sorry if we appear to have got off to a bad start. I always struggle at this time of year; childhood shit I won't go into now. So, one of you tell me what you have, while I bring a pack of mince pies over,' Charlotte said as the atmosphere in the room relaxed and Nash explained what they had to date.

Charlotte listened and didn't make any notes while Nash spoke.

Finally, Nash addressed Charlotte, who appeared vacant but had been concentrating.

'What do you think? Dr Miller?'

'Sorry. From what you've told me about the choice of weapon and victim, I don't have much to go on at all. I don't mean to be rude but surely you can see that?' she said as she glanced at them both over her coffee cup.

'I'm not certain that it isn't random. There's nothing from what you've said that would lean towards a woman, and because the person you arrested said it was a man he'd met, there could be bias. But he may have told you that just to keep you at bay and to not push him further into a corner. He may have nothing to do with your case, of course. No disgruntled mistress that we know of?'

'None. All avenues we've explored show his only vice was gambling in the private card school. Early analysis of his computer shows that he doesn't visit sites of concern. All legitimate Islamic sites concerning faith and the Qur'an. Some are about gambling and fending off addiction. Emails showed no concerning traffic or correspondents either and certainly not another woman. His phone records also correlate with his computer use. What we have is a man of faith, murdered on a London street,' Nash summed up.

'Well, unless you get more evidence for me to go on, then I'm not going to be of much use beyond a generic profile, which won't help at all,' Charlotte replied as she slipped off her stool indicating the meeting was over.

Moretti and Nash thanked her for her time as they were shown out.

CHAPTER FIFTEEN

Moretti remained in his car in the car park of the marina. After leaving Charlotte's, and dropping Nash off at the office, the day had gone slowly with little else moving forward. Nash had the intelligence desk working up the information they had on the name Gary, and enquiries were underway concerning the address. The voters register and DSS were both unhelpful in getting any surname for the resident. The observation point officer was reporting no movement at the premises.

Nash had told Moretti she'd decided to staff the OP during the day then go to a remote camera feed for the evening. She didn't like the idea and it wasn't her first choice, but her budget was dwindling, and she needed some reserves for when the suspect got nicked.

He could see the lights were on in his boat and he assumed Tabatha must be up or had left the lights on for him.

It was ten o'clock. He'd stayed in the office and laboured over more statements trying to figure out where they could go next.

He thought back to what Charlotte had said. She'd texted him after the meeting saying she was sorry if she came across as hostile, but it was a shock seeing him despite the prior warning.

She'd also hoped he'd get in touch again and they could catch up properly over a drink. Whatever that implied was the last thing on Moretti's mind.

He exited his car and slung his coat over his shoulder as he made his way towards his boat. Despite his tiredness he was in no mood to sleep. The door was locked and as he put the keys in to open it, there was resistance. He tried again and realised Tabatha had left her keys in the other side. He tapped three times and waited. It wasn't long before he heard the lock turn and the door opened slightly. Once she saw it was Moretti, she opened it.

'Sorry, Nick. I was getting showered and felt vulnerable. Plus, I'm sure you wouldn't want to walk in on me walking around your boat naked?'

Moretti smiled politely but ignored the question. She wasn't naked now but dressed to go out. She wore slim fit jeans, a white blouse, and a huge black and white chequered scarf that enveloped her neck like a boa constrictor. A black leather jacket finished it off.

Moretti felt sad she was leaving as he could have done with chilling out with her.

'Work or pleasure?' he enquired as he hung up his coat.

'Work, unfortunately. Pleasure is a distant memory,' she said.

'Well, maybe we could do something once I'm finished up with this investigation and you get a night off?' he asked.

'That would be great.' She kissed him lightly on the cheek and left the boat. The last thing Moretti saw was her walking up the gangway and the back of her knee-length black leather boots shining in the outside movement sensor light. He took a beer out of the fridge and undid the screw top cap.

Tabatha had been working on her painting and he stood, slugging a drink from the ice-cold bottle, and marvelled at her artistic talent. He'd never been much of a creative preferring to exercise the logical side of his brain. Much of his childhood was spent building Lego, adding engines, and progressing to self-build radio-controlled cars. He had a model boat he was creating in the study. A work of love crafted from balsa.

He decided now would be a good time to revisit it as he needed to relax his brain in the same way Tabatha would at her easel. He flicked on the light to the study and the boat was as he'd left it on the desk. The hull complete, he now needed to concentrate on the sails. It was a modern sailboat, as he had no interest in the ships of yore.

As he placed his beer down on a Met Police coaster, he noticed a Post-it note attached to the side of the ship. It just said "nice work! T ;) x". His houseguest had been looking around then. Not that it bothered him – he had nothing to hide, no skeletons in the cupboard that would cause major fallout if news spread beyond the confines of his boat. He gently peeled it off and stuck it on the side of a metallic penholder.

He liked that she'd taken an interest in what he was doing, and she didn't consider it lame. He wondered just how long Tabatha planned on staying as he hadn't had the chance to ascertain the situation with her own home. He wasn't looking to evict her, but he'd have liked to know where he was at, and hoped she'd be staying until he got back from the holiday he had planned for after Christmas, as an inhabited boat was better than a vacant one. He wouldn't be the first to return to uninvited crew.

At the same time, he felt the holiday was becoming more of a fantasy than reality with every hour that passed.

* * *

Appeal boards were out on the street, social media was being exploited, the Superintendent had done an appeal on both local TV and radio and yet, nothing. Silence. Not even the snouts were reporting whispers.

This led Nash to believe the killer was either a lone wolf or not from this part of London. She'd requested that all Met police source units task their sources in case they'd heard any talk, but didn't hold out much hope on a response. She was relying on the individual handlers to task their sources and she knew the likelihood of that was minimal, especially around Christmas when parties were in full flow; even the sources needed some downtime.

A predator with a desire to slaughter out on her streets was not a situation that sat well with her or her team, all of whom were getting restless with no leads, some already waiting for a new job to break or an old one to have some activity. To Nash, any unsolved murder was a negative mark against her. She'd earned her rank but knew that Crockett and Tubbs who oversaw all her investigations were waiting for her to fall on her sword.

They were both men of a prehistoric mindset that saw murder investigation as the work of men. Nash knew that for all the messages the service put out about equal opportunities there would always be someone higher up the chain of command who'd only paid lip service to the doctrine. Fact was she'd already showed them up in her dedication to duty and detection rates. She could only work with what she had but she desired a clean sheet for her team.

Her team had gained a reputation for getting the job done and the command had recognised this, as the Commander had spoken to her about promotion to DCI.

CHAPTER SIXTEEN

Howard Jameson's svelte physique moved with the gait and motion of a mountain goat. He'd alighted the bus at the crest of Crouch End Hill and continued on foot towards the Clock Tower. This evening his energy felt good despite the rigorous afternoon of bible study he'd endured. He checked about as he made his way towards his idea of heaven while he dragged an overnight case behind him. Its wheels had seen better times. The daypack he had over his shoulder slipped and he hunched it further up his frame to prevent it falling. His wife had told him he didn't eat enough and that if he continued the sparse diet there'd be nothing left of him to enjoy. He ignored her protestations with a beatific smile. A smile she hated.

He reached the junction with Coleridge Road and avoided a couple in a push and shove outside the King's Head. He crossed and stopped outside a main door next to a Costa Coffee. He pressed the bell, checked his surroundings again. A click sounded, and he pushed the door while he pulled his case over the threshold. He closed the door behind him.

A while later he was heading back downstairs. Jameson wouldn't have left the comforts he'd been enjoying if he knew he was going to die. Definitely not when it was to obtain fleeting pleasure from more alcohol and a bag of weed. He stood at the base of the stairs and faced the door that would provide his exit at street level. He pulled down the handle and the door opened a crack. His conscience told him he was on a different mission from the one he'd been destined for and by doing so ensured he checked the Broadway left and right before he stepped out. As he closed the door and looked up at the glow of light from an upstairs window, his feet detached from the earth and he went to meet his maker.

He was slammed against the wooden door from behind. A gloved hand wrapped around his jaw and mouth and prevented him from shouting. All he managed was a muffled whimper as he twisted his body in vain to evade his captor's grip. He sensed the warm breath of his assailant by his ear and felt powerless to do anything as he opened his eyes and his sight locked onto the black polished blade that feathered over his nose and chin until it finally came to rest at his throat.

A knee that dug into his right hamstring shifted position to the side. He gave a final swallow of life as he felt the pressure of a sharp edge against his throat. The edge of the blade sank a millimetre before it gained depth and found its line of passage across his neck, severing his jugular. He felt the hand at his head release and move to his front trouser pocket and his head dropped forward as though severed from a string that held it up. His last vision as he slid down the panelled door was of his key in the Yale door lock that jangled in a light breeze against the chipped paint.

CHAPTER SEVENTEEN

Nash attempted to open her eyes, but they resisted and remained shut. She fought the will of her nervous system until the resistance finally acquiesced. She wiped saliva from the edge of her mouth as she lay still and stared at the ceiling. She gradually came to realise the buzzing sensation that entered her dream in the form of a large swarm of flies in a dark room was in fact a real sound.

The buzzing became louder and the frequency in sound it elicited finally broke her resolve. She scooped her hand back and forth under the pillow. As she pulled her phone out, the buzzing got louder. She looked at the screen and it displayed "contact desk".

She pressed the green button. A gruff-sounding male's voice filtered through her head.

'DI Nash?'

'Yes,' she answered in a low tone.

'Sorry to bother you, ma'am.'

That's the first lie, Nash thought, as the contact desk was doing their job of calling the person with the responsibility of dealing with a case. That person they'd correctly ascertained was her.

'Another murder's been called in by night duty. Body found outside the Costa Coffee, Crouch End Broadway. Uniform are on scene reporting a male with a slash wound to the throat. Shall I leave you to call a HAT car out?' the operator said.

'Leave it with me. Send me through the details via phone and email. Thank you,' Nash replied. She finished the call then rang Moretti.

He answered on the third ring. He sounded groggy.

'Oh, come on, Pip. I've just got to sleep,' he moaned.

'Sleep's for the weak. Get the HAT car down to Costa Coffee, Crouch End Broadway. We have another body. I'll see you there, bring coffee in one of your many Thermoses until we can blag one when Costa opens,' she said as she counted down from five in her head for him to bite.

'Get your own, you earn enough,' he replied.

She gave it ten minutes then called him again. The phone rang four times then it was answered.

'I'm up. I'm up,' he said.

* * *

Nash arrived shortly after Moretti. She parked up at the edge of the outer cordon that uniform had put in place. It was a large cordon, which she appreciated. She'd rather start with it big and move it inwards once they had everything they needed than start small and risk losing evidence.

She displayed the logbook in her car and put on her protective clothing for the scene. A new tent was in place and the area was calmer than at the mosque. It wouldn't remain that way for long as rush hour was approaching. The high street was on lockdown with diversions in place for traffic. Despite the time, there was already an interest in the arrival of cops. There was always that person who never slept. That person, who insisted on keeping the scene guard officer company by the tape, never failed to show up.

She signed the PC's log and walked towards the inner cordon where another uniform stood enveloped in a scarf that covered his face revealing only his eyes. He looked tired. Nash sympathised as the temperature had dropped to minus two and being stood still took effort in the cold. She signed the second log and entered the tent. Moretti was present along with the SOCO who'd examined the previous scene.

The victim was a skinny white male, mid-forties, dressed in dark linen trousers, white shirt, brogue shoes, and a quilted down jacket.

His hair was thinning on top. He'd fallen forwards into the door of a flat that was over the premises. The blood spatter on the door glistened in the street lamp's light as Nash watched a rivulet of blood slip down a groove in the wood.

'Shit,' Nash exclaimed as she adjusted her step from treading on it.

Moretti handed her a small exhibit bag that contained a wallet, various IDs, and business cards that had been separated from it to ascertain who he could be.

'This is all from his jacket. I haven't been able to check anywhere else yet. It looks like a similar MO, Pip. The jugular has been severed and by the look of the blood spray so has a carotid artery this time. Waiting on photography, then Dr King who's been informed and on his way. No witness, as such, but there's a woman inside pretty shaken up as she heard the victim slamming into the door. She came downstairs and opened it and was presented with him. The victim had been with her and was leaving her flat to get more drink. She's identified him as Howard Jameson to the PC upstairs with her. I haven't seen the woman as I've concentrated on down here,' Moretti said.

'OK. Carry on with what you're doing. I've spoken with some of the team. George will get the HOLMES system up and running and a few more will be down to assist you with early house-to-house and CCTV. I'm going upstairs to speak with this witness,' Nash said as she stepped through the open door to the outside hall and climbed the stairs to the top-floor flat.

Her suit crunched as she walked. She pulled down her facemask as she reached the flat's door which was ajar, so she softly tapped the frame with a torch she'd been carrying. A young PC came through to her. She showed her warrant card and introduced herself.

'She's through in the living room, ma'am. One thing before you go in…'

Nash pulled the door open and motioned to the officer to step away from the entrance. 'Yes?'

'Well, it's kind of awkward…'

'For you or her?'

'Well, not me, but…'

'Fuck's sake spit it out, I've got a body outside and the public waking up.' As soon as she'd expressed them, she regretted her choice of words. The officer's uniform appeared too clean and new for Nash's liking.

'Sorry. The victim's a priest, our witness has been having an affair with him for the past six months and's now getting concerned that he's dead outside her flat when he was meant to have been on a conference in Brighton,' the officer finished.

'Well, that was simple, wasn't it? Trust me…?'

'Darren.'

'Darren. I've heard much worse and nothing shocks any of us in my position. In the future, just tell it as it is. Come back in with me and introduce me to…?'

'Karen… Karen Sharp. Well that's the name she gave me but there's something not right about her. I've not been doing this job long and if I'm honest, I feel a bit out of my depth,' Darren replied.

Nash nodded in appreciation of his honesty.

'Well, Darren, sometimes we all feel that way despite how long we've been doing this job. So, why don't we get to the bottom of why you feel the way you do? After you.' Nash motioned with her right hand for Darren to lead the way into the flat. As Nash stepped in, she noticed the place was nicely decorated, pop art style pictures on the wall, none of family or anything personal. She followed Darren along the short hallway. The kitchen to the left was neat and looked unused. She had a brief look to her right and in a room opposite she could see an unmade super-king-sized bed. Satin bedspread crumpled on top of clean-looking linen; Egyptian cotton, she bet herself. The spread matched the mulled-wine-coloured padded bedhead.

Karen Sharp was sat on a settee and smoked a cigarette from a silver holder. Her hands were unsettled. The deep-red nail polish reflected in the silver gilt of the holder that quivered around her mouth. She took a long drag before she looked in their direction. She had long, dark-brown hair and appeared to Nash to be in her mid to late thirties. She wore a silk dressing gown that left nothing to the imagination, bare legs and feet curled under her.

'I'm Detective Inspector Nash, Homicide Command. I'd like to ask you a few questions, if I may?' Nash sat opposite Karen and the PC sat next to her at a kitchen table.

Karen looked at Nash. 'I don't suppose I have much choice, Inspector? I can't add much more to what I've said already. I saw nothing.' She took another draw on her cigarette and crossed her fake-tanned legs as she adjusted her dressing gown.

Nash removed her latex gloves and held them in front of her. 'I understand the victim had been in your flat before he was killed?' she asked.

Karen shifted again. Nash knew this wouldn't take long.

'As I said to the young copper here, he'd been here for a few hours and was leaving to go and get some drink then go home.' She eyeballed Nash as she replied.

'He's a friend of yours?' Nash probed.

'Yes. We knew each other from a night school class we were taking, modern art, at a college in Holloway.'

'So why was he here in the early hours of the morning? You did say he'd been here a few hours?' Nash asked as Sharp shifted, uncomfortable at the way Nash questioned her.

'What does it matter, Inspector? I've told you he was here, he left, and was killed. It wasn't me if that's what you're implying?' She leaned forward, stubbed out her cigarette, and opened a silver cigarette case from the low coffee table which was sat on a Vivienne Westwood Union Jack rug. Nash had wanted one for her flat but didn't have the thousand pounds plus to burn.

'I'm not implying anything of the sort. I need to establish why he was with you before he was killed. I appreciate it's been a traumatic time for you,' Nash said as she attempted to build rapport.

'It's been more than fuckin' traumatic. I could be next. What if he was being targeted or something?' Karen snapped as she drew her dressing gown tightly around her.

'You're getting way ahead of yourself… sorry, remind me of your first name again? I don't think you mentioned it?'

'Karen… Karen Sharp – no "e",' she replied with a slight smile.

'Karen, I need to know everything about him. You can help or hinder me, but I will get to the truth, I always do. I believe you have something that's bothering you that I may be able to ease your mind with.' Nash looked at her as she turned away and stared out the window. A window she'd spent many a day looking out of in a daydream of a better life.

Outside was getting brighter, the street lights setting off the glint in the frost-covered windscreens of the stationary cars. The cigarette shook in her mouth. Nash took the lighter from Karen's hand and she let her light it for her. Nash placed the lighter on the table as she sat back.

'Is this your flat, Karen?' she asked as she leant back in her seat and surveyed the room.

'Yes,' she replied with a degree of hesitation in her demure tone.

'How long have you owned it?'

'I don't own, I rent. Who can own in London nowadays?' she replied with a brief laugh.

'Tell me about it,' Darren said, proud he'd been able to join in.

'The artwork's all yours?' Nash asked as she looked at the walls.

'Yes, of course it is. I don't rent that. Where's this all leading?' Karen bent forward in Nash's direction.

Nash blanked her as she feigned further interest in the property's artefacts. 'The artwork in your hallway… what's the title again? Damn my memory's poor this morning,' Nash said as she gently slapped her forehead.

'I… I can't remember either; can't we just get this done? I've got a busy day ahead and I'm not an art gallery for your entertainment,' Karen said.

Nash knew she'd had enough as she got up from her window seat. Nash put a hand up for her to remain seated and Karen did as she requested.

Nash mirrored Karen's seated pose as she bent forward and cradled her latex gloves like a comfort blanket.

'Thing is, Karen, I don't think this is your flat. I think you rent it, but for your work. That artwork in the hallway isn't yours. You'd know if you owned a limited-edition silkscreen print from a set of seven by the artist Peter Blake. They're titled *Motif Ten* by the way. It's funny how certain details can just come back to you, isn't it? How's your memory now, Karen? Oh, I'll need some ID from you too – passport, driver's licence, or any other form of photo ID.' Nash finished speaking and sat back, satisfied that her work there was complete.

Karen couldn't watch her. Her expression changed from one of pity to one of defeat. Nash waited, using the silence to her advantage and hoped Darren would keep his mouth shut.

'All right, super-cop, so you've busted me. What now?' Karen asked as she messed with another cigarette and re-lit an incense stick, the ash from which dropped into a wooden holder.

'Just start again and this time tell me exactly what the situation is here. That way I can work with you, as I don't wish to work against you,' Nash explained as she turned to the PC.

'Officer, can you ask DS Moretti to come up here please? You've done enough, thank you.' Nash looked at the PC whose pupils were dilated and appeared confused at her instruction.

He got up and left them and Nash waited for the familiar sound of Moretti's feet. She didn't have to wait long but enjoyed the silence as she could sense Karen had used the time to weigh up how honest she intended to be.

They heard a light tap on the door, a rustle of forensic suit, and Moretti entered the living room.

'You need me for something? Oh, hello, Monica! Long time, no see? How's tricks? Oops, wrong expression, sorry, love.'

Moretti sat down and smiled at Nash. Nash was happy that Moretti's days in Vice hadn't been wasted and confirmed what she'd suspected the set-up to be. Monica aka Karen let out a resigned sigh.

'I'll make us a tea, shall I?' Moretti suggested as he rustled towards the kitchen area while Monica let her head hang and took a large intake of nicotine, exasperated at the thought she'd have to start all over again.

CHAPTER EIGHTEEN

The immediate scene was under control and the body had been removed. Nash brought the team back in to be briefed. She waited for everyone to settle with his or her respective drinks and notes. They'd had a busy start and deserved a breather.

'Thanks for coming back so quickly. I appreciate we're all knackered, so I'll kick things off with what we know so far. The victim is a trainee priest by the name of Howard Jameson. He's married, with two teenage kids, no previous convictions. He'd been visiting our witness for the last six months. Last night was one such visit. The witness initially gave her name as Karen Sharp but is in fact Monica Lewis. She's an escort who rents the flat above Costa Coffee on the Broadway, N8. Jameson had been on a "visit" and was leaving when he became our second victim. We're linking the two. It's an identical MO.' Nash paused while the officers assimilated what she'd said. She let the cacophony of voices settle to a murmur before she carried on.

'Monica can only give limited information. She's not an eyewitness. Intel – in addition to the standard research I need to know everything about the witness, Monica Lewis: who owns the flat, who leases it, how much, cash or cheque, who else visits? Everything we can get on her, I want. That goes for the victim, too. Let's see if there's any link between Hussein and Jameson. We need to expand the search criteria for this weapon now that traditional routes are proving negative. Jameson's family have been informed of his death. His wife and family are being looked after by Lucy who's FLO for this investigation. Lucy.' Nash cast a glance at DC Lucy Pendleton giving her the stage.

'Thanks, guv. I haven't got long as I need to be back with the family, but they asked for some space as it's been a busy morning for them. His wife, Amanda, has identified the victim. She insisted she needed to do this sooner rather than later. She's naturally upset as she thought he'd stopped it all. He's got history for visiting sex workers. She wasn't surprised he wasn't where he'd said he would be. He'd told her he was going to a conference in Brighton and given the hotel details where it was purported to be taking place. She never believed him but didn't say anything. She'd phoned the venue Jameson had given, and the conference wasn't even listed – poor skills, I say,' Lucy said as Nash looked up. Her eyes told Lucy to keep her opinions to herself despite those being Nash's thoughts. Lucy shrugged by way of apology and continued.

'Other than that, there was nothing of concern raised. A man of God who enjoyed sex way too much outside of the home,' Lucy said.

CCTV, house-to-house, press appeals, forensic collection and testing, and statement gathering were all ongoing. The intelligence staff had nothing further to add at this stage but were hard at work on the profiles Nash had requested. Nash was about to wrap up the meeting when Lucy interrupted. Nash nodded for her to continue and she waited for the room to calm down.

'I don't know if it's relevant or not but the victim didn't play cards. According to his wife he was a shagger but not a gambler,' she said.

Nash looked at DC Pendleton and her forehead creased as she squeezed her eyes as though blinded by the sun.

'Good of you to ask the question, Lucy, but when I said the same MO I meant in terms of the jugular being cut not that the victim played cards,' Nash said with genuine warmth as she never discouraged questions.

DC Pendleton looked around and appeared confused.

'I know that, ma'am. I know what MO is, it's just that I asked her about the playing card that was found in his trouser pocket when he got to the mortuary and was searched before his clothing was bagged up, as I thought it might be relevant and a line of enquiry similar to Mr Hussein,' she said as though Nash was aware of this, which she wasn't.

'What type of playing card was it?' Nash enquired as the other officers all turned in Lucy's direction.

'Same as the one found on Mr Hussein, an ace of spades.' A brief silence loomed over the room as the details were digested. Nash broke the silence.

'Nick, get the cards to the lab. I need to know if they are from the same type of pack and if there's any DNA or prints on them that may help us identify who's touched them. Jonesy, I want you to go to the card school and seize the pack they used. Take some money from the imprest and buy them another if needs be. I need to know if either card came from that pack or not. I appreciate that most gamblers would use a new pack but this isn't a typical situation we're dealing with and these cards may be unique in creation. Our killer doesn't play by the rules. I just need to rule this angle in or out. I also need to know where it was bought from, when, and if there's any CCTV of who purchased the pack.' Nash's mind was churning over with the information from DC Lucy Pendleton. This could break the case wide open.

'Right, we'll have another meeting later. In the meantime, I'm off to the post mortem and a Gold Group meeting with two Borough Commanders and the Assistant Commissioner. You don't need me to tell you that the various faith communities are getting skittish. If it gets out the second victim was a man of faith, then this will only add to the mix. Let's keep it wrapped until I say it should be released. I can't control the victim's family and friends but, Lucy, I want you to speak with his wife and tell her to maintain a silence as far as any press requests she may get. You bat them off or contact me and I'll do it. OK, let's get back to work and find this killer before they strike again,' Nash said.

With that the occupants of the room left.

* * *

Nash stood outside the North London mortuary in Tottenham and took in some fresh air. The result was as she expected – a similar killing to the first. The pathologist,

Dr King, confirmed what Nash already knew, but it still came as unwanted listening once it was officially recorded. The victim had been standing facing the door and looking up when the blade had cut. Dr King would only go as far as saying the blade used was similar to that used on Mr Hussein. Once he'd looked under the microscope at the wound he'd have a better idea whether to increase his maybe to a strong possibility. Nash had contacted her DCI and updated him they had another identical murder. Nash didn't like the term serial killer as that provoked a host of problems she didn't need. The national media being the main one.

The incident room had already received calls from people claiming they'd done it, not to mention walk-ins at police stations claiming the same thing. All took up valuable resources as they couldn't be ignored. No, she could do without all of that shit. Her DCI assured her he'd try to supply all the extra resources she would need. The will was there but the likelihood of any further help when the murder rate was going up in the capital was slim to none. Two murders in a short space of time and only her team to deal with them.

DIs on other murder teams had stopped calling each other asking for extra staff as no one was going through a dry period as far as new cases were concerned. The increase in knife crime had only added to the problem.

The bitter trill of her phone interrupted her moment of serenity.

'Nash.'

'Boss, we've had word back from the SOCO. She wants to see you back at the scene. I'll text you the address.' Adam Moody, a young DC from the intelligence desk, sounded tired.

'What for?' Nash said.

'Didn't say much other than it's a rooftop,' Moody said.

'Call me should anything else come up,' Nash said as she hung up and called Moretti who answered on the third ring.

'Meet me outside the TSB in Crouch End. I'm in Tottenham but I'll cab it over to you. The SOCO wants us. Something about a rooftop,' Nash said.

'I'm about ten minutes away,' Moretti replied.

* * *

'So here we go again then,' Nash mused as Moretti alighted from the taxi, balancing a drinks tray, and sidled up to her outside the TSB bank on the Broadway. Last-minute shoppers ram-raided butchers and artisan craft shops. Moretti made a mental note he needed to get something for Nash. She looked after him at work and he knew he would have been back on Borough with a less tolerant DI.

He knew she hated Christmas from her constant disparaging remarks whenever they saw a set of outside decorations. He equally knew she was in the same position as him, alone at a time of year when it was expected you'd be with family or invited by friends to join them. They always volunteered to be on-call at this time of year. Let others of the same rank who had children take the time off to be with their kids and loved ones. They would then disappear on holiday as soon as the children were ensconced back at school and holiday prices returned to an acceptable level. Moretti would be abroad on a beach while Nash opted for the open roads of Scotland on her motorbike.

'How are you now you've fully woken up?' Moretti asked as he handed Nash a takeout hot chocolate, which she gratefully accepted.

'Oh, you know, never happier than to be investigating a pile-up of bodies before Christmas while freezing my tits off in Crouch End surrounded by crazed shoppers and crap festive lighting, you?'

Moretti took a sip of his drink and adjusted the collar of his coat. A merino wool scarf kept out the worst of the December chill.

'Always cup half empty with you, hey, Detective Inspector?'

Moretti moved his feet and warmed his hands on the cardboard cup.

'Well, it's not like I've got a hot stripper to keep me warm on a winter's evening, is it?'

She winked. Moretti bit.

'She's not a stripper. She's a conceptual artist who happens to remove her clothes as part of the act. Anyway, I have an electric blanket for warmth and that'll do me,' Moretti replied while he concentrated on his drink and observed the distance between where they were standing and the place the victim dropped.

He wondered what the SOCO wanted them for. They would soon find out as behind them, the SOCO's van arrived. The SOCO walked over to them looking in windows as she carried her box of tricks.

'And where's mine?' she said as she looked at their cups.

'Nick got them in. His mind's on other things at the moment. Well, two other things to be precise,' Nash remarked while trying not to laugh. She stared at Moretti who shook his head at her feeble attempt to wind him up.

'I don't want to know. Shall we go and see what we can find?' the SOCO asked as she walked ahead of them.

Moretti nudged Nash's arm as he passed her, just enough to cause her to slop hot chocolate down her coat.

'Missed your mouth, Inspector? I'm most surprised.' Moretti laughed as he followed the SOCO and left Nash wiping down her jacket with a gloved hand. As she caught up with Moretti, she playfully pushed him in the back.

A uniform officer shuffled around as he clapped his gloved hands together. He stopped as he noticed them approaching. He hadn't seen Moretti or Nash before, but the SOCO aside, he could tell by the walk they were detectives.

'Took your time, didn't you? I see the detectives looked after their own as usual?' the PC quipped in good humour as he looked at the cups they carried. A career uniform beat officer who had two years' service left to do before retirement and spoke as he found it but without any animosity or malicious intention towards any of his superiors.

'Not the police staff, I hasten to add,' the SOCO said as she smiled and suited up along with Nash and Moretti.

Moretti took out his wallet. 'Here, I can't take any more of the whinging, go and get you and her Powdership here whatever you want but make it quick. The DI with the stained coat will have another cocoa as she had an accident with the last cup, so make sure you get a tight-fitting lid, you know, much like the one you're wearing,' Moretti joked.

Moretti handed over a twenty. The PC laughed and accepted his gesture of goodwill. Moretti ordered a bacon roll for himself and an egg and cheese for Nash. He knew he'd have time to kill while the SOCO examined the roof before calling them up.

Too many feet spoil a scene and he knew from the council CCTV operator that there wasn't a body on the roof that required immediate medical aid. The SOCO disappeared while Moretti and Nash waited at ground level. She'd examined the hole that had been cut into the chain-link fence across the fire escape at the side of the Town Hall. Some fibres had been present which she collected.

The Town Hall was alight with festive trees and sleighs that provided the ideal shield from anyone looking up to the roof. A large tree in a grass area to the front also masked the view from the ground up. Nash hoped the CCTV from the council would provide some image of their suspect and was desperate for the call that confirmed something, anything at all, to give them a clue as to who they sought.

Despite Charlotte's summation that it was likely a man, Nash was keeping an open mind. Plenty of women were expert in the art of cutting with a knife and with so many soldiers returning from active war campaigns to a life on civvie street, she wasn't ruling out a crazed or disgruntled soldier let down by life. Weak, she accepted, but a hypothesis at any rate. She made a mental note to contact Charlotte following this second attack. She knew what Brown had talked in his interview about the person he'd met being a man, but she also accepted Charlotte's view that Brown may have been lying, or that this had nothing to do with their investigation. However, to Nash, it was unusual for someone to go to the lengths the person had gone to at concealing their identity. Never in her time as an undercover officer had someone been so cautious. A false name or sending someone else to negotiate was the preferred way. The fact that he had bought a knife that sounded like it fit with Nash's investigations couldn't be dismissed.

The PC returned, burdened down with a cardboard cup holder and paper bag. He handed Moretti some loose change. The SOCO called them within thirty minutes and that told Nash all she needed to know. There was nothing of immediate forensic value up there. They left the PC where he was and went to the roof of the Town Hall.

'Over here,' Yvonne, the SOCO said, gesturing as she spoke, her voice muffled through the facemask she wore.

They followed her to a low wall, and she pointed out the view. A clear and unobstructed line of sight to the window Monica was looking out of when Moretti had broken her cover. The same window the killer could have been looking into when Jameson was getting ready to leave. The street door was also in plain sight.

'There's nothing of any forensic value coming back from the first scene, at least not yet. I hoped the killer may have made a mistake up here and that's why I called you. It could fit with the previous crime in that they like to observe the victim from up high before they descend to kill.' Yvonne paused and reflected.

'For what it's worth, I'll have all the photographs ready as soon as possible. There are some more fibres on the stone wall and it's a guess, but if the killer leaned on it while they watched the victim in the window it could've come from their clothing. I'm guessing though. I know that doesn't help and I know I've lectured on how I work on evidence not supposition, but you never know. Oh, and they've not made the same mistake of stepping in cat litter or soil this time, sorry,' she said as she finished packing up her kit.

'I'll be available for any others, Pip; my supervisor is good with it too. Better for continuity and if I'm honest it's better than another burglary,' Yvonne said.

Yvonne left them on the roof as they stared out across the Broadway. Nash dropped her mask from her face, and it hung around her neck like a windcheater. She sat at the edge of the low wall that surrounded the roof edge. She pictured the suspect, prone, waiting, cool, calculated, and cold-blooded. The tree masked the street's CCTV camera from what Nash could see but there were others that may have captured the suspect getting up to the roof.

One benefit to this time of year was there were no leaves to obstruct the line of sight.

Moretti joined her and they sat awhile, each in thought.

'It's a fucking nightmare Londoners don't need. If the press gets hold of this and link the two, we'll be under even more pressure to make an arrest quickly,' Nash said.

Moretti nodded in agreement. She wouldn't rest until she had a name on the charge sheet. The right name on the sheet. As they sat, Nash's phone rang, and she accepted the call.

'DS Nash, homicide.'

'Boss, it's George. Just had a call about the outside OP on the address we were given by Lee Brown; no one left the building last night and no one's returned. That's from both the camera at the front and rear. Thought you'd want to know,' George said.

'Thanks, George,' she hung up and told Moretti the message.

She thought for a minute then said, 'Right, let's go and break the fucking door down.'

CHAPTER NINETEEN

They waited for the call from DC Jules 'JJ' Jackson to tell them that he had obtained a section eight warrant to search the address. JJ had tried his hand in the fraud squad but decided the life of a detective on a murder team suited him better. He was a black guy who had the build of a middleweight boxer and wore his made-to-measure suits like a model. He was Moretti's go-to detective when he needed a message to be enforced. His sheer size, cool manner, and presence was usually enough to assuage the most hostile of suspects to calm down and become cooperative. It wasn't that JJ emanated an aura of hostility, he didn't. He was as laid back as they came. He was also a dab hand at writing the information required for a warrant and presenting it at court. A skill few cops were getting the opportunity to practise out on Borough due to the high demands from day-to-day policing with little time for pro-active work.

* * *

The tree-lined street they went to visit no longer presented the leafy vista it displayed in summer. Each tree had unburdened its dead. The naked branches swayed in the breeze as Nash sought a place to park a reasonable distance from the address they needed to search. She found a space and took it, performing a textbook reverse park.

The address was a ground-floor flat within a Victorian terraced house in a residential street. They had no official key to let them in this time, so they'd brought one the Met used to access most properties in London. The enforcer or the "Big Red Key" as it was known within the force.

With it came JJ as he had the warrant and the training to use the thing. Both Moretti and Nash watched as he unfurled his frame from the non-descript job vehicle. He made the Volvo XC60 look like a Mini. He was suited and booted wearing a puffa jacket, beanie, and woollen gloves. He popped the boot, took off his gloves, and replaced them with a set of gauntlets that protected his hands and forearms. He then lifted the sixteen-kilogram steel tube from the boot and as he closed it, slung the enforcer on his shoulder with the same ease he'd lift his grocery shopping.

'This the door, boss?' he said as he walked towards them.

They were stood inside a small front garden the path of which led to the door of the flat. Nash smiled at JJ's humour. Despite where they were stood, he still wanted verbal confirmation from the lead rank at the scene that this was indeed the correct address before he hoofed the door off its hinges. He knew it was as he'd done a recce and double checked the research he'd been given prior to obtaining the warrant. It wouldn't have been the first time police had got it wrong and forced entry on innocent occupants.

'Yep, this is the right door,' Nash replied, with a nod.

JJ reciprocated the acknowledgement and with two strides stepped up to the door and dropped the ram from his shoulder. He took hold of both handles weighing up the enforcer as he did. He turned back to where Nash and Moretti waited.

'You're gonna want to stand back. If I get it wrong, then three tonnes of pressure could come flying back towards you,' JJ said.

Once Nash and Moretti moved back, JJ loosed the tube and sent the door flying inward with one stroke of the steel.

'There you go, boss. Here's a copy of the warrant. I need to be elsewhere now unless you need me here?' JJ said.

'We need the same on the flat door to the premises?' Nash said.

'Of course! It's been a long few days, Pip,' JJ said.

With that they let him lead the way. By the time Nash had stepped over the shattered glass and splintered wood of the main door JJ had done the same to the flat's.

'I'll call someone else on the team to handle my enquiry. I'll wait until it's good here. You never know who could turn up,' JJ said as Moretti tapped JJ's sculptured shoulders in appreciation at his slick work.

'Wait here. There's no point you getting forensically dolled up. Besides, we're running out of your size,' Nash told JJ as she and Moretti donned the protective over suit and boots. They entered the flat sticking to a common approach path out of habit more than anything.

The flat consisted of a living room, kitchen, bathroom, and bedroom. It was in the bathroom that they both stopped to take in what they'd been presented with. A slew of joker playing cards had been arranged to look like water running from the tap, forming a pool of cards at the base of the bath. All faced up. Jokers staring back at them, mouths open in laughter displaying comic teeth.

Someone had prepared for their visit. The quality of the cards looked good from what they could see. The high gloss reflected the white of the bath. Nash bent close and could see the card they were printed on was the depth and overall size of a standard playing card. The same quality as the ace of spades cards found on the victims.

'We're going to need to get Charlotte, officially, on-board. You know that already, though, huh?' Nash said, turning to Moretti.

Moretti remained still, transfixed by the vision in front of him.

'Jesus, Nick, this is one sick bastard we're dealing with and I have to say, I'm kinda feeling a wee bit out of my depth with this one, so yeah, let's get our favourite psych in and see what she has to say,' Nash said as JJ appeared in the bathroom doorway after thinking it was too quiet in the flat for his liking.

'Whoa! This shit just got real, eh, guv?' he bellowed.

'You got that right, JJ,' Moretti replied.

'To be honest, I think I'd rather be seein' another body than this weird shit,' came his muffled response through the face shield he'd put on along with an undersized suit. He'd got bored playing guard.

They moved outside the door to the flat. The house was now their crime scene. The upstairs flats were unoccupied. As they sat on the stairs and waited for the SOCO and the search team, Nash's phone buzzed in her pocket. She rolled down the forensic suit and answered it.

'Hi, Pip, it's Adam from Intel. Sorry it's taken so long to get back to you. I needed to double-check everything before I called. I've found a link: all the properties involved in both murders are controlled by the same letting agents. All of them. I've double checked and even the one you're in now is run by them.'

'Good work, Adam. Text me the details for the agency, get on to whoever got the keys for the first place we searched and find out who he got them from, will you? We need background checks on everyone from the agency with a focus on links to the victims. Finally, tell the DCI he's on his own for the Gold Group meeting. I'm busy right now and he can call me later should he need to.'

They said their goodbyes and hung up.

The search teams arrived. This time Nash knew they'd have more to go on. If Lee Brown had been honest, then their suspect must have been in and out of the flat and that would mean they'd have left a trace they could work off. Nash felt the suspect must have got sloppy at some stage. No one was perfect after all. Especially when it came to crime.

She'd leave that to the forensic lab and Charlotte to confirm or rebut. While she remembered, she sent Charlotte a text to arrange a meeting and quickly. She pressed send and it showed as delivered but not read.

She could feel a trickle of sweat down her neck despite the coolness of the flat and the outside temperature. She felt an increased awareness of being out of her depth despite her years of investigative experience at the highest level. This case was not the norm. She hoped with this one that once she had a forensic lead or new intelligence, she'd trace and arrest the suspect quickly. Her job. Her investigation. Her responsibility to apprehend this killer and bang them up for life.

* * *

Outside, the uniformed sentry became distracted by a car. His focus shifted to the vehicle as it cruised away. A figure dressed in a black winter coat, dark woollen hat, black jeans, and black Doc Martens boots walked past the entrance. The uniformed officer stepped back to let the person pass while he continued his watch on the vehicle. The person nodded their thanks at the officer. As the figure neared the gate, they glanced across and saw the damage to the door.

The figure rounded the corner, stooped and re-tied the lace of one of the boots. As they crossed the final cord, a house key slipped through their fingers and disappeared through the slat in a drain cover before they carried on walking away from the police.

CHAPTER TWENTY

Nash scanned the morning paper. There was a brief mention of the murders, but it related to her witness appeal. It was 8 a.m. She tapped the cap end of her pen against the top of her blue counsel's notebook. She checked her watch. He was late. DCI Carlson was never on time; there was always one drama or another that required his attention before he could start a meeting. She heard the main door to the landing open and the unmistakable sound of shoes on the tiled floor. His aftershave was the next thing she noticed.

'Sorry, Pippa. The tube was running late,' Carlson offered by way of apology. Nash waited for him to take off his coat and scarf and get settled. He brought out his own shop-bought notebook and closed the door.

'OK, well, the Commissioner has been in conversation with a representative of London's Jewish community this morning,' Carlson said. 'He demanded to know if the rumours about a serial killer were true and what were the police doing to reassure the community? If that wasn't enough, they would appear to know this person is targeting religion or, more to the point, two people who happened to be significant within their own faith communities. The representative, rightly, in my opinion, believes his community could be next in line. It's not good, Pippa, not good at all. I know you and your team are doing all that can be done but there must be something we're missing? Something that we can work on to get this killer banged up before they kill someone else.'

Carlson paused and settled into his chair, book open, pen readied for action. His gut strained against a tired belt and caused his belly to make an appearance through a spent button.

Nash sensed the true purpose of the meeting was beyond an update from the Gold Group. Carlson was here to ensure the shit he'd received was passed down to her. She was in no doubt the Assistant Commissioner had delivered the Commissioner's message loud and clear: *Sort this out and fast. We don't want vigilante patrols up and running all over London.* The community representative had also told the AC he would encourage increased security at schools and synagogues. Nash had no issue with that and privately considered it a wise option.

'I can tell you exactly where we are to date, sir,' Nash said as Carlson waited for the situation report. 'Tracing a manufacturer for the knife let alone establishing the type of knife we're dealing with is proving to be quite a task and won't happen anytime soon. Whoever our killer is, they are meticulous and a planner. I believe there's victim selection taking place and these haven't been random hits; it's one draw of the blade, one kill, on each occasion. The throat area is the target and the jugular in particular. On Hussein they missed a carotid artery so the bleed was minimised to a large pool of blood. On Jameson they weren't so lucky and they hit a carotid artery and it sprayed everywhere. My feeling is that panic set in as the kill site was very open by comparison to that outside the mosque. We have also established that the properties tied to the investigation are all linked to a letting agency. Enquiries are in hand there.' She stopped and flicked through her notes while Carlson continued writing.

'The playing cards left at the scenes are an anomaly. They're with the lab. I'm going to need to bring in a forensic psychologist to help with that. Look at an offender profile, why the cards are being left and what the message is by leaving them there. To date, we've had an ace of spades left on each victim, and in the flat we raided this morning there'd been a creation of sorts – Jokers –

made to look like water running into the bath.' Nash paused again and waited for Carlson to finish his written notes.

'The cards are a weird angle, that's for sure. At least we know that the flat you raided today is associated with our suspect as the press don't know about that. It would appear the information Lee Brown gave had some credibility to it. Get the source unit to visit Brown in prison and lean on him again. He's had more time to think now and may be ready to spill some more,' he said as Nash made a note of the action.

'The psychologist, sir? Can I get one on-board?'

Carlson put his pen down and looked out the window.

'Same one we used on the Connelly case? Charlotte, someone or other? Was she any good, Pippa?'

'She helped make sense of a possible motive, although not one hundred per cent accurate, it was good enough for me and we got a life sentence for murder,' Nash said, as convincingly as she could.

'Very well. Have her sign an inclusion notice and be wary about what you share, from an investigative standpoint, that is. Now, I have another meeting to go to but keep me updated on how the letting agency visit plays out and any new forensic leads. Make sure you task the source unit today, Pippa. Time's not on our side,' he said.

With that, Carlson collected his belongings and left her office, not closing the door. She was about to get up when Moretti appeared.

'I've called the source handlers from downstairs and they're on their way up,' he said.

'Thanks. I've messaged Charlotte but she hasn't got back to me yet,' she said as a cough came from behind Moretti and she turned to see one of the source handlers had appeared.

It was the DS of the unit this time, which could only mean he'd be requesting overtime out of her diminished budget. DS Hugo Dillon was triathlon fit with a softly spoken northern accent. He stood at over six feet and had a liking for scarves, reminding Nash of Johnny Depp, but that's where the similarity ended.

'*Ciao.*' His first word as he strode into the office and sat down. Nash noticed the number of fabric bracelets that encased his wrists had increased and wondered if he'd just been deployed at a music festival. Nash liked him because he was a grafter and if he said he'd do something, he would.

'Good of you to come. I'm up to my eyes in work and I need a prison visited and a potential spoken to,' Nash said, as DS Dillon listened to what he saw as a demand rather than a request.

'As it happens I was coming up anyway to suggest we do a follow-up visit on your man, Brown, get an update as to where you're at and how we might approach the next meet.' Dillon sat back, his hands out in front of him palms up.

'Like hell you were coming up here for that, Dillon. Don't forget I know you of old. You don't shift from where you happen to be sat unless it's to your advantage or someone has put a rocket up your arse due to your team's inactivity. I'm surprised to see you, it's been so long I thought you'd taken early retirement,' Nash replied with a smile.

Dillon laughed. 'I miss the banter, Pip. Good to see you're still as dry as ever. Look, I'll get the fella a visit. We'll go over what he told us before and try to prise more out of him. No promises though,' Dillon replied.

'Good. Look, I'm keeping things close right now. See what he comes up with and feedback anything as soon as you can by phone. Don't wait until the ink dries. Plus, rally your other sources up too. If one of them can name the guy doing these kills, then they're in for a good payday.' Nash finished speaking and got up. Dillon did the same. After Dillon had gone, Moretti and Nash left for the estate agents.

They hadn't phoned ahead to the agents. They both preferred the element of surprise for this visit.

'Can we turn this off?' Moretti enquired as they sat, stuck in traffic, Nash nodding her head to Idles' *Mother*.

'Why? Didn't have you down as a musical prude,' she replied.

'I'm not, it's just that listening to some guy shouting "mother-fucker" over and over is doing my head in,' Moretti said as he looked for the mute button to press on the car's entertainment system.

Nash reached over and slapped Moretti's hand away. He concentrated on the outside world.

'What other sounds do you have?' he asked as he dropped the glove box and searched for a CD.

'It's the radio. I have no say in airplay. Despite my exalted status on the team, some things are out of my control. You might want to remember that,' she said.

Moretti started pressing buttons on the radio skipping Classic FM, R4, R1, R2 then left it on XFM as an advert played out.

'How much further?' Moretti enquired.

'Christ, it's like having a three-year-old in the car. Not far now.' Nash gave him one of her playful smiles.

They came to a set of lights and stopped as they'd changed to red. As she did the radio DJ queued up the next track – Motörhead's *Ace of Spades*.

'Great track!' Nash said.

'Whatever, more your idea of music than mine,' he replied. He looked about as the opening bars vibrated the door pocket speakers as Nash cranked it up.

The lights turned to green and Nash moved off towards their destination. Moretti stared at the radio. He leant forward as he listened deep in concentration. A look Nash only ever associated with him when they conversed on the tube.

'You a fan too?' she asked as they crawled along.

'Pull the car over!' Moretti demanded as the track faded out.

'All right! Keep your hair on, what have you seen?' Nash asked as she unclipped her seat belt in preparedness for a foot pursuit. It wouldn't be the first time she'd been out with Moretti and ended up in a foot chase. He was the kind of cop who attracted trouble and couldn't leave it alone even when they were in the middle of a job.

She saw a bus stop up ahead and pulled in.

'Well…? Nick?'

'The words, Pip, the words to that song…' Moretti drifted off. His brow creased; eyes squeezed tight.

'Classic, I know, but that was a somewhat extreme reaction to a pretty old anthem as far as heavy metal goes,' Nash replied.

'No, no, no, the words, Pip, the fucking words… they… they… where's your phone?' Moretti demanded.

'Here. Why?' Nash handed him her own iPhone.

'Have you got that track on iTunes? I need to listen again,' Moretti said.

'That's like asking Dolly Parton if she's got a country and western playlist. Of course, I have,' Nash replied as she took back the phone and accessed the track.

'Play it, play it again,' Moretti said almost at the point of excited delirium.

'Nick, are you OK? What's going on?'

Moretti stopped his concentration and looked directly at Nash, his face visibly relaxed as he spoke.

'Just play it and listen to the words, will you,' Moretti said. He sat back, pushed his fingers through his hair and ran them over his stubble while she found the song on a Like-it-Loud song list and pressed play. They listened. As it got to the end Moretti looked at her.

'Well? You must understand now? The connection to the ace of spades playing cards at the kill sites?' he asked her as a bus pulled in behind them and the driver flicked them the middle finger as he passed, as he couldn't park properly for his passengers to get on and off.

'Look, I heard the lyrics but other than the title matched the song I don't get where your mind's gone, if I'm honest. Sorry to burst your euphoric bubble,' Nash responded.

Moretti palmed his eyes and continued down his face. As his hands passed his lips his mouth was one huge grin that revealed a good set of teeth. Nash waited then had to speak.

'So, you're telling me the killer made a radio request to XFM, for *Ace of Spades* to be played? *For all the detectives currently working on the Playing Card murder here's Motörhead's Ace of Spades?* You need to get some sleep, Nick, you really do,' Nash said.

'OK, smartarse, I'll let the expert decide,' he said as he called the intelligence desk and requested a blown-up copy of the lyrics be printed and left in her office.

'Let's go see the letting agent,' she said as she motioned for Moretti to turn the music up.

CHAPTER TWENTY-ONE

'How can anyone afford to rent or buy anything in London?' Moretti asked Nash as they stood outside the letting agent's window and browsed what was on offer. Moretti was comforted in his choice of floating accommodation. It wouldn't suit everyone, but Moretti didn't regard himself as a run-of-the-mill punter. They continued looking in the window and waited for the space inside to become occupied. A light was on and it appeared open despite the absence of any staff and a locked door.

A man appeared from a side room. He could be seen through the advertisement boards as he shook the hands of a couple in their thirties. As the couple exited Nash and Moretti took the opportunity and entered.

'Hi, I'm so sorry but I have to dash as I have a viewing booked. Did you make an appointment? Mr and Mrs…?' The agent looked at them both. Nash removed her beanie and gloves.

'We're not together nor on the lookout for property. We wish to speak to the owner, a Mr Peterson, Neil Peterson. That wouldn't happen to be you, would it?' Nash asked.

'Who's asking?' the agent replied as he stuffed a property flyer in a laptop-size leather grab bag.

'DI Nash and this is DS Moretti, Homicide and Serious Crime, that's who,' Nash fired back.

'I see, well, you'll have to come back, DI Nish as I'm off out,' Peterson said.

'It's Nash and your visit can wait.'

Peterson wasn't in agreement. To him a potential sale or let was everything in a market that had become increasingly competitive. Peterson was a born and bred Londoner and he had no intention of having his arrangement disrupted just because two cops waltzed into his establishment and demanded his time. He ran a tight diary and prided himself on being punctual, even if his clients weren't of the same mind as him.

'Look, if this is about a traffic violation or parking fine I haven't paid, then you'll have to come back. I'm late or at least I will be if I don't get away now as my last meeting overran. Carrie, my receptionist, will be back soon and she can book you in for another time this week but we're closed soon for Christmas so you may have to come back in the New Year when we re-open,' Peterson replied.

They both watched as Peterson began to put on his Armani winter coat.

'Mr Peterson, this isn't a visit I'm going to reschedule. I'm not here about a traffic violation. I'm here about two murders…' Nash let that hang.

Peterson listened but continued to fasten his coat. 'Well, as awful as that sounds, I'm afraid I know nothing about any murders so if you'll excuse me,' he said as he made for the door.

'Sit down, Peterson. This isn't up for debate.'

'Make it quick,' Peterson said.

Moretti kicked a wheeled office chair towards Peterson who trapped it with his foot and sat down as he stretched his thirty-two inch inside legs out, arms behind his head.

'Well? What is it you need?' Peterson asked.

Nash stood while Moretti perched on the edge of the only desk in the makeshift space Peterson called a 'client reception area.'

'I need to know who has access to a couple of properties on your books,' Nash said.

'So, you think I should hand that kind of private information over to you, just like that?'

'Yes,' Nash responded, bluntly.

'DI Nash, I run a tight and professional ship. Respect for my clients' confidentiality is at the very top of my agenda. I don't care what you're investigating. I won't pass over private information without a warrant or legal authority of some sort.' Peterson remained laid back while he stared at Moretti then Nash. Nash moved closer to Peterson, which caused him to straighten up.

'I heard there were still cops like you left. Ones who think brute force and intimidation will get them all they want.' Peterson pushed the chair back with his foot in a vain attempt to escape Nash's casual encroachment. His exit failed as the back of his chair hit the internal doorframe causing him to drop forward with an unexpected jolt.

'Mr Peterson, Neil, I'm not the officer you've made me out to be, in fact I'm one of the most amenable in the force, isn't that so, Sergeant?'

'She's right. Very approachable, personable lady,' Moretti replied with a full smile.

'So, I assure you I'm not here to cause you or your business clients any problem. But, and it's a big but, I'm in the middle of a murder investigation, two in fact, where property you own and or have control over have featured. One in particular where I believe my suspect may have either lived or accessed,' Nash said.

Peterson remained where he was, no more than two feet from Nash's face. Moretti's eyes drove into Peterson with the intensity of a lion about to kill his prey. Peterson swallowed as Nash continued her speech.

'So, if you'd be so kind as to provide the details, I'd be obliged.' Nash brought out a folded piece of paper from her inside pocket and handed it to Peterson.

Peterson took it and ferreted in a drawer by his desk. He retrieved a set of reading glasses. Nash gave him some space as Peterson viewed the paperwork she had supplied.

Peterson looked up and rubbed his chin as he read through the addresses again in an effort to bide time.

'I've been hasty in my resistance to your reasonable request. I can tell you that the only people who have access to those places are the tenants, aside from the one here, as it's vacant,' he said pointing to the first site the killer had been to.

'What about this one?' Nash pointed to the address they'd searched earlier. Peterson typed in a command to the computer. His index fingers drummed a pattern on his desk as he waited for the information to appear on screen.

'Odd, just a minute,' Peterson said as he tapped some more on the keyboard and pressed send.

Nash and Moretti moved to get a better view of the screen. They could see an information sheet arise and the address details, but the other personal fields of information contained the name Mickey Mouse, and a date of birth of 01-01-1965. Peterson pressed a tab for account details and the details showed sequential numbers for both sort code and bank account. He turned to Nash.

'I'm telling you; I'm as confused as you are. This shouldn't be... I mean obviously it shouldn't be here... I...'

'Who else has access to this computer?' Nash enquired.

'Me, I have access. That's it. This is a secure area. For my eyes only. Wait...' Peterson went into his drawer and got out a key to a large filing cabinet behind them. They gave him some space as he opened a lock and pulled out the bottom drawer. He retrieved a file with an address on and opened it. As he did an A4 colour picture of a joker drifted out and landed on the floor. Peterson bent down to pick it up and Nash grabbed his wrist.

'We'll pick it up,' she said, as Peterson sat back up.

Peterson shifted back as Nash retrieved a set of latex gloves from her jacket pocket and without putting them on, pinched the paper within the latex and placed it back in the folder it had fallen from. She then placed the folder on Peterson's desk as though it were about to explode.

'Well, Mr Peterson, looks as though we're going to be here a lot longer than we first envisaged. Your agency is now my crime scene,' she said as Peterson threw his hands atop his head, his eyes set on the folder on the desk in front of him, his cocksure demeanour reduced to one of bewilderment and confusion.

CHAPTER TWENTY-TWO

The search and forensic examination of the letting agency didn't take long. The joker had certainly been an unexpected turn up for everyone concerned, most of all Peterson, whom Nash didn't believe for one minute was her suspect. Nash had formed this belief on seeing his reaction to the cartoon details in the tenant entry sections on the computer as well as the sequentially numbered account details. Peterson had been keen to show her everything once this had surfaced.

Other accounts appeared legitimate on the face of it but Nash had the tech boys image Peterson's hard drive so they could dig further in a hope to see when the details were altered and, if possible, by whom. Nash accepted it was a long shot but in the world of murder investigations, you explored every opportunity for evidence. Peterson had also provided a list of past employees and those who had accessed the office, which didn't amount to six. It would seem Peterson was a reasonable man to work for and staff turnover wasn't an issue. He was a man who liked to deal in cash where he could and avoid the taxman.

Peterson had taken Nash to one side and confessed the situation with Monica's flat – that she paid cash and he asked no questions.

He categorically denied knowledge of how she earned her money. He'd received no complaints about her but didn't expect any as it was a flat above a shop that opened at six thirty in the morning and shut at seven at night. Nash had listened but offered nothing by way of reassurance. She knew Peterson was being economical with the truth as far as having no knowledge of Monica's employment was concerned.

According to Monica, Peterson was a regular client. Nash had a way with words and a quick call to Monica was all it had taken to establish the set-up. Both Nash and Moretti were aware they shouldn't ignore it but right now wasn't the time for additional complications in the investigative cauldron. They needed Monica to remain where she was while the enquiry ran its course. Tracing her as a witness for court would prove troublesome, as she knew how to disappear when or if she needed to.

An appointment had been made to meet with Charlotte. Moretti didn't wish to go but Nash insisted he must as she needed to see if Charlotte agreed with his theory that the lyrics linked with the investigation and their killer's state of mind. Two heads were better than one when it came to evaluating what Charlotte would come up with. Moretti held back on his thoughts in the car as he knew if he tried to explain it, it wouldn't make sense but he got the instinctive feeling he was onto something and he would express his views in a report Charlotte would read.

'Why the reluctance with the psych visit?' Nash asked as she signed off the exhibit logs.

'No reason, just that I've got so much on, I could do with the time to complete my actions,' he replied.

Nash knew that was a lie as she'd seen his actions and they amounted to very few by comparison to others'.

'I don't buy into that for one second; so let me reassure you. This is a professional visit. The DCI's approved her employment so she'll know there's money coming,' she said.

Moretti nodded at Nash's unwanted explanation. He longed to just be on his own, out and about doing what needed doing and not having to engage in conversations about crime or staff issues. He also realised this was unrealistic now there were two murders to investigate.

A silence continued between them as Nash closed the logs. Finally, it was Nash that broke it.

'Shall we go?'

'Sure,' Moretti replied.

CHAPTER TWENTY-THREE

They reached Charlotte's house in good time and Moretti rang the bell. This time the door was answered quickly.

'Hi, please come in. Go straight through to my office. It's the only room off the kitchen,' Charlotte explained as she waved them both through.

Moretti wiped his feet and Nash did too. They walked through to Charlotte's office and sat in single seats. Charlotte's desk was in front of them adorned with a phone and A4 notepad only. A bookcase displayed an assortment of texts pertinent to her role. Certificates of training hung from the wall in bold frames. Nash wondered what Little Miss Mind Doctor would make of Moretti's report. Charlotte returned with coffees on a tray and sat at her desk. The mugs were Le Creuset. A matching set.

Moretti knew he'd never pick these up in his charity shop hauls.

They all took a cup and Nash kicked things off.

'Thanks for seeing us again. As I explained on the phone, I've spoken with DCI Carlson and we'd very much like your professional assessment based on what we know about our target, I mean, suspect, at the present time.'

Charlotte nodded. Nash slid a sheet of typed paper over and Charlotte put on her reading glasses and read through the wording, tracking each line with her fountain pen as she read. She signed the Memorandum of Understanding not to disclose anything they discussed beyond their group. Moretti brought out his report from his man-bag and handed a copy to Charlotte.

'Take your time looking through the report. We can discuss anything you need to know once you've read it,' Nash said as she picked up her mug and scanned the room. Charlotte immersed herself in the paperwork.

As was the case in these situations, the room remained silent save for the sound of a page being turned or the clink of a spoon in a mug. Moretti dumped three sugar cubes in his and dispensed with the milk. He felt the need for a full-on caffeine hit and the sugar would only add to the overall experience of keeping him awake and focussed.

Charlotte took her time and both Nash and Moretti waited patiently. After a while she finished and set the file down. She rubbed the bridge of her nose and sought a tissue.

'Well, you've certainly picked up a bad one, that's for sure,' Charlotte said. Nash restrained herself from comment. 'Both victims have a religious connection albeit with different faiths, but each faith has a belief in a god, and I think that's important here.'

'Why?' Nash asked.

'Every faith has a list of rules, commandments, or precepts. Ideally, these rules must be adhered to or there are adverse consequences. Both your victims have broken at least one of these rules in accordance with their faith. Your first victim did by gambling and your second with sex outside of marriage. I believe this is significant in the killer's victim selection,' Charlotte replied.

'The issue of the playing cards is the most interesting thing and something I haven't seen before. Often the suspect takes trophies like clothing, jewellery, or some other object personal to their victim, but it's not as common to leave a trophy for police to find. It's as though the killer has offered the cards as some kind of prize for the discovery of a new part of the puzzle, even though they're adding to the puzzle by doing so,' Charlotte continued.

Nash had her pen and blue book perched on her crossed thigh and made notes as she spoke. She glanced up at Charlotte once she'd finished talking, conscious not to miss any point she made.

'Just as a card player would keep his or her hand away from the other players, the killer is putting theirs on open display. The killer's way of getting your attention, above and beyond the bodies they left. Having fun while they taunt you. Making the murders a game of chance, which is ironic, really, as the victims they have selected are anything but. Quite a sick individual, if you ask me. Whether the message is a personal one or directed at the service as a whole is too early for me to say. Nevertheless, the suspect is toying with you and that's of grave concern to me,' Charlotte said as she took another drink before adding another sugar cube.

'Why's that? You're going to have to expand on that theory,' Nash pressed keen to make headway.

'Forgive me. I will get to the lyrics you supplied. I do agree with your theory of a link between the song *Ace of Spades* and the playing cards of the same name that have been left at each site. It fits. As farfetched as it all seems it sits well with me,' she said as she looked at them both before she continued. 'The cards of the joker are another matter though. To me the use of this card isn't a form of mockery, as the image would suggest; it's a warning. A warning of further deaths to come. Now, Detective Inspector, before you come back at me with another "why?" I will explain.

'The killer is craving attention. We can see that from the use of the playing cards and the overt nature of the murders. The cards are left out in the open, albeit on the body, and not hidden away where they could lay undiscovered. They knew you'd find the cards. If they didn't wish to be discovered, then why kill in this way? Why not just kill inside or dump the bodies where the police wouldn't discover them for some time or dismember them for that matter and scatter the parts across the country. I digress, my apologies.' Charlotte stumbled with her words. Both Nash and Moretti made no comment and waited for Charlotte to regain her train of thought.

'There's no forensic evidence, so far, that links to any known suspect. But whoever the killer is, they have some forensic awareness beyond the average person. They are enjoying the attention and no doubt getting a buzz out of watching you run around after them. Every time you make a move, they know; hence you win a prize. The card's a reinforcement tool designed to give you some credit that you're making progress.' She paused then continued, 'The question is, progress towards what end? What final reward? Redemption? They haven't finished whatever message they've set out to send or, more to the point, they haven't had the reinforcement or answer they require to make them stop. I hope I'm wrong, I really do,' Charlotte said, her face turned towards Nash.

'So, you're saying they will kill again but you can't say who our next victim could be, but the MO will be the same?' Moretti asked.

'Correct. I'm not a seer, Nick. I can only go on what you've presented. My professional judgement is based on what I've been shown. Nothing, so far, gives me any indication as to what section of the faith community they will target next. All I can say, with ninety-five per cent certainty, is that they haven't finished. As for MO, I would expect it to continue in the same pattern, but nothing is certain.'

'How can you come to that conclusion? You've told us they are close and must know where we will go next by the cards they leave so why not just stop now? Game over, go abroad, and keep their head down?' Nash asked as she shut her book.

'It's all in the lyrics to the song,' Charlotte said as she opened up the file and took out the lyric sheet Moretti had provided. They all gathered around the printed words as she continued.

'With the first victim the clue's here, in this line about greed: win or lose it's all the same to him. He doesn't share their greed. The killer abhorred the act of a Muslim man going against Sharia law by gambling. It doesn't make the killer a Muslim, it does make the killer a person who bides by rules of faith, even when those rules are ones they break, as in *thou shalt not kill*. To the killer, their actions amount to a purification of sin. In their warped world they're the only person who may rid society of sinners by purification through death.' Nash and Moretti remained silent and let Charlotte continue.

'The next line of significance is here: *Playing for the high one, dancing with the devil*. The killer has shown your second victim that by dancing with the devil, aka Monica, they were game on for death. *Thou shalt not commit adultery* – sex is the sin and the sinner must be purified. He's showing how it's all a game to him, as in the lyrics, as this is how the killer is viewing it. But it's a deadly game with serious consequences for those who break the rules. In the mind of the killer, Jameson was called by God to perform a role as a priest. I wouldn't be surprised if when you find the killer, they claimed that a higher power willed them to rid the world of these people.' Charlotte took a sip of coffee and tied her hair back using a scrunchy that was wrapped around her slender wrist.

'The final act of the play, if you will allow me that expression, is this. They have doubled up but haven't quit. Hence killing twice in succession. They're having too much fun. The killer knows they will lose in the end and they don't wish to live for much longer themselves, just as the line in the song states, *I don't want to live forever*.' Charlotte stopped. Her face paled and she appeared to have become withdrawn.

Both Nash and Moretti shot each other a glance. A look they both interpreted to mean something was being left unsaid. Nash spoke up.

'Whatever's on your mind, just get it out, Charlotte. We're not here for a definitive solution to the enquiry; we just need a different perspective and an idea of our killer's personality and possible motive,' Nash said, hoping to reassure her.

'It will end when the killer chooses to lead you to them — *I see it in your eyes, take one look and die*. I just hope it's their death and not yours.'

CHAPTER TWENTY-FOUR

Another day done and Moretti left Nash at the office. A driving sleet tested the fast wipe on Moretti's job car. He should've pulled over as the visibility was poor, but he was conscious of the need to be home and near a reliable phone. The conversation with Charlotte's had caused him much consternation, especially the last thing she'd said. Nash wasn't buying into it all and on the journey back to Hendon had claimed some of it was all psychobabble and bullshit. But she'd respect Charlotte's credentials and would work with what she'd presented.

Moretti reached the gated entrance to the marina. He swiped his access card and the gate drew back letting him through. The ground, now covered in a white mush, prevented him seeing the painted white lines that denoted his parking space. He decided to abandon his car where it had stopped. Good luck to any would-be thief in this weather.

He mentally gave a three count and bailed out of the car, the keys to his boat in his right hand as he leant into the wind and wet and moved towards the boat's access light. To Moretti, the light felt like a beacon of warmth. He wondered whether Tabatha was in. It was only 9 p.m. and he hoped she was out. He was tired and just wanted to crash with a Scotch and The Bad Plus on the turntable.

He reached his own front door. He bashed his shoes against the boat to dislodge some of the muck that had accrued on the sole. As he went to insert the key, the door opened violently. Tabatha pulled him in by his jacket collar. He felt powerless to react.

'Thank God you're back! I was getting concerned you could be stranded. Sorry for, you know, pulling you like that. Just relieved you're safe,' she said as she put her arms around his waist and hugged him, her body side on to his. She let go. Moretti stood, unable to move due to the confined space of the porch he'd built and the unexpected display of affection. His planned evening of jazz and serenity was screwed.

'I haven't had a welcome like that in some time,' he said. 'How was your day? I hope you were warm enough? I need to order more heating oil and logs for the burner.' He stumbled through each question as a way of deflection from the display of warmth he'd been shown. He shook out his coat before he attached the neck loop to the hook, dropped his bag, and kicked off his shoes. As he entered the boat, he could hear jazz from the living room. Miles Davis and not Moretti's album.

He entered a vista that was a cross between midnight mass and a séance. Light danced from the whitewashed walls thanks to the multiple candles placed on every available flat surface including the edge of the floor. They cast a warm glow that filled the minimalist space.

Tabatha had been back to her boat. She wore loose paint-daubed denim dungarees set off by a white T-shirt. Her hair was tied back in a short ponytail and Moretti struggled not to stare at her natural beauty. The T-shirt rode up at her midriff and exposed a lean, tanned, stomach. What were obviously her albums lay stacked against the turntable's cabinet. She noticed him looking at them.

'Sorry about those. I'm not moving in, I promise. It's just that the boat's getting condensation and damp with the heat off and I'd hate to lose them to the elements. Anything else I'd cope with the loss of but not my music collection. I saw you had LPs too and was hoping you'd understand?' she said.

He went over to the fridge, took out a beer, and offered one to Tabatha who accepted. He knocked off the bottle tops using the worktop opener he'd attached. He went over to where Tabatha had been painting and sat on a perch stool she no longer required as she stood to paint.

'If you've got anything else that needs protection then bring it over. It's not like I don't have the space. How can you work when the light's so dim in here?' he asked as he nodded at the canvas that was still on the easel.

'Don't you like candles?' she asked with a look of hope.

'I find them practical. I never knew I had so many though,' he said as he looked about the floor.

'You don't. They're mine. They're great in a power cut and with the weather the way it is, I thought they could be useful. There's a delay in the boiler being fitted and it looks like I'll need a new heating system throughout the boat,' she said quickly as she stared at the painting.

Moretti heard what she'd said but didn't comment as he preferred to watch her paint rather than discuss how long the proposed works to her boat would take and how that would impact on the length of her stay.

'I see that guy's killed again. You're not dealing with that case, I hope?' Tabatha asked as she reflected on the depth of blue required to complete a section of her painting.

'I am,' Moretti said as he moved away and slumped into an easy chair near the wood burner. The heat from the fire was welcome after the bitter chill outside.

'They say he's going to kill again, well that's the fear, anyway,' Tabatha announced.

'Typical. I've been so busy I've not caught the news and I'm not one for the front of camera appeals. I leave that to my boss. She loves the limelight,' he said.

'I think you'd be very photogenic, myself. Is that the lady who was here the other night?' Tabatha said as she turned to him.

'That was my detective inspector. She's my immediate boss but it's my DCI who's the camera lover.'

'Oh, I see. I was offered film work once.'

'Oh yeah, did you train as an actress?'

'I act every night I'm at the club. Nah, this was porn and I'm not interested in going there. It's one thing getting your tits out on stage, it's another getting everything out on camera and being abused for others' pleasure and entertainment,' she replied.

Moretti sipped his drink unsure of where the conversation was headed. He'd seen enough porn to last him a lifetime and not in a good way. He'd worked child protection where he'd had to view banks of monitors all of which showed porn to ascertain what offences were being committed. All of it depraved. He didn't care much for porn of any kind after that.

'You're not working tonight?' It was the best response he could think of to change the subject but show he'd listened.

'No. To be honest, I don't know whether I'll be going back,' she responded.

'Oh? You been having problems there?'

'What if I had? Would you be going in there to sort them all out for me?' she replied as she stood, paintbrush in hand, palette in the other.

'Not my area of expertise. That's licensing, not homicide,' he said and smiled at her.

'Well, never say never,' she said, laughing, as she mocked someone being stabbed with her brush. 'It was the way your inspector looked at me when we met the other night. It made me think about how I was making ends meet. She was mocking me; I know that, I heard her. It was written all over her face the way she looked at me and then at you, you know, in judgement at my life choices.'

Moretti put the bottle down and got up to get another beer.

'She can be indiscreet at times, but she has a heart of gold. Not that it justifies the way you perceived her actions to be,' he said as he looked in the fridge.

'I've lived my whole life being judged by others, so it felt empowering at the time to take control. Doing what I chose to do despite how outrageous that seemed. I earn good money there, treated well by the boss, no hassle, and good tips each night. Get the right punter in and they'll give away hundreds just for a wink and a seductive smile. Madness, if you ask me,' she said as she turned back to her picture and swiped the brush across the canvas.

'How long have you been working at the club?'

'About a year. As soon as I get enough cash to pay off my student debt, I'll stop. Who knows where I'll go after that, abroad maybe,' she mused.

'What did you study?' Moretti asked as he noticed how the picture had developed since he last saw it, that and how beautiful Tabatha appeared in the light of the candles.

'Painting at The Royal College of Art. An MA. I have a first degree in computer science but wanted to move away from creating code to working with paints.'

Moretti sipped his beer and lay back on the sofa while he stared out of the reinforced glass skylight he'd had installed. The idea was to provide some connection with the outside. Fat lot of good it was tonight with no stars to view and just a constant stream of white that covered every inch of the panel. Tabatha interrupted him in his thoughts.

'Have you always been a copper?'

'Yes. Since I was nineteen. Left college and joined up. It's all I've ever known and all I ever want to know. I guess I'm lucky to have found my passion and still enjoy what I do,' he said as he sipped the beer.

'Even when you deal with death every day?'

'It's an honour to bring those who kill to justice. There's no other feeling like it when you hear the jury return a unanimous verdict of guilty and the defendant gets a decent prison term, nothing better. That goes for any offence not just murder, mind you,' he said as he glanced over to where she stood.

'So don't you have any empathy for those that are struggling and have to steal to feed their family or those on the poverty line trying to make their way in the world abiding by the rules but when they slip up through need, all the police ever say is, "bang them up"?' Her voice had taken on a direct tone that wasn't lost on Moretti. It wasn't rude, just opinionated and forceful.

'Let's just say anyone who was like that that I've come across professionally, never made it to court. Some of us aren't without empathy, you know?' He stayed as he was, looked at the ceiling, and wondered whether tonight would be the killer's next foray or whether the snow would stop play. He closed his eyes and listened to the gentle scrape of bristles from Tabatha's brush on the canvas and the sounds of Miles Davis. Slowly his eyes closed, and the empty bottle slipped from his fingers.

* * *

He awoke the next morning to the vibration of his phone against the boat's wooden floor. He was still on the sofa, fully clothed but a blanket had been laid over him. The candles were all extinguished and the white sheet of snow now lay thick on the skylight roof. He picked up his phone and saw it was 7 a.m.; his caller a withheld number.

'Moretti,' he said in a low voice.

There was a brief silence at the other end and Moretti was about to repeat himself when the caller spoke.

'We haven't met… well, we have, but not how I'd like. You're getting close now, shame about the snow. I was looking forward to meeting you properly, up close and personal; just you, Nick, or is it Nicholas? Tell anyone of this call and others will suffer the same fate as the last barbarians… until we meet then?'

Moretti sat up. He looked at the phone's screen and saw the call had been ended.

He stood up with the blanket around his shoulders, the voice on the line still in his mind. It had been muffled by some kind of voice distorter. He screenshot the call details and saved the image to his photo roll.

'Fuck!' he shouted into the void as he sat back down and held his head in his hands. He rested the phone against his forehead. How did this person have his number? He was glad it was his job phone and not his personal one but still, it wasn't a public number.

As he sat, he realised he'd shouted when he had someone on the boat. His spent bottle of beer was on the worktop in the kitchen. He got up and moved about slowly as he went and checked on Tabatha. He felt the need to ensure she was all right.

He stood outside the door to the spare room and listened. He could hear nothing. The door wasn't shut and presented an inch gap. He pushed it and looked in. Her bed was empty and unmade. Maybe she was up and in the shower? He went to the bathroom but again the door was wide open. He checked the remainder of the barge and realised she wasn't there. He suddenly turned with a jolt as the barge door opened letting in a swirl of light snow.

Tabatha kicked the door fully open as she stood with two takeout drinks and a brown paper bag in her mouth that contained something greasy judging by the now translucent bottom. Moretti took the bag from her mouth.

'Thanks, I was wondering how I was going to manage,' she said as she brushed past him dressed in his Berghaus arctic parka.

They were both now seated on the sofa he'd slept on. Tabatha dumped his coat on the floor beside her. She was appropriately dressed for the weather.

'I couldn't sleep last night and after you'd fallen asleep on me, well not literally, you know what I mean... I thought you might appreciate a decent coffee and breakfast before work,' she said.

'Very much so, thanks. Sorry for falling asleep last night, not a usual habit of mine.'

'That's fine. At least I know where I stand.' She mocked as she took a drink, adjusted the plastic carryout lid so the slot met her mouth.

CHAPTER TWENTY-FIVE

'Can't you do the main office?' Nash shouted towards the cleaner who'd decided it was the right time to hoover her room just as she was about to phone the lab. He lifted his headphones and Nash repeated herself. The cleaner nodded and exited dragging the Henry hoover behind him. Nash closed the door. She could deal with the low hum of the vacuum as the cleaner resumed doing the hallway.

She'd got the tube into the office given the weather. The inside team were, as always, huddled over screens.

Nash was blanked by the lab and decided to hang up. She got up and looked out over the parade square as Moretti slid on a layer of snow towards the entrance to their building. She turned back and circled her head as she tried to relieve the tension in her neck.

A knock on her door brought her back to reality. The Silverfox from the source unit framed her doorway, a sheet of A4 in his hand. He either had something useful to tell her or he carried it to give the appearance he had a sense of purpose and was busy. The former was the case.

'Can I come in?' he asked.

'Sure. Close the door. Coffee? I've just fired up the brain juicer. I don't know about you, but I fail to function without this stuff,' she said as she walked to the clear glass pot, removed it from the heat tray and poured out two mugs of black nectar. She handed one to the DC and sat in a comfy chair at a low table.

'Check this out.' The DC passed the paper to Nash who scanned down it. She was quick at first then her eyes began to slow.

'This is good?' Nash said.

'It's sound, Pip. For your knowledge, our friendly has seen a photo of the knife, dated yesterday, with the middleman in the same image. Not touching it, I hasten to add.'

Nash took her blue book from her desk and made a note before she passed the sheet back to the handler. Another knock at the door and this time it was Moretti.

'Come in and shut the door behind you,' Nash requested.

Moretti had decided not to mention the call he'd received just yet, afraid the killer would act on his threat. He tried to keep the conversation light.

'Do we have some intelligence from the source unit? That'd be a first,' he said in jest. It was a common source of banter between them and taken in good humour despite the DC's roll of his eyes. The DC handed him the A4 sheet and Moretti read through it then looked up.

'This is good?' he asked.

'Yes, it's good. Don't any of you trust us to do our jobs?' the Silverfox enquired of them both.

Nash and Moretti responded unanimously with a smile. 'No.'

Nash continued, 'So, when was your person asked if they wanted to buy this knife?'

'Last night. They'd heard about the murders and thought they'd better call me first before they agreed to anything. I've just taken the call, or I'd have belled you yesterday evening,' he was quick to confirm.

'So, what now?' Nash asked him.

'Well, my friendly has spoken to the middleman to get the weapon. The middleman says it's a handmade knife that's the sharpest they've experienced. Trust me, my friendly would know as they've been stabbed a few times in the past. The handle is carved and the blade's darker in colour than the usual steel ones. It's been designed to kill, not to whittle wood or peel your apple. That's all they know.' He spoke with a sense of satisfaction that can only come from a good day's work.

Nash sat, pensively, fingers steepled.

'Let's set up a buy and see if we can get the knife and the seller, it will need to be quick though, like today,' she said.

The Silverfox's head craned back in laughter. His hands covered his face. Moretti knew why. Any action that involved the Undercover Unit was never quick. The chance of getting anyone to go and buy a knife today, let alone this week, was remote as it was so close to the twenty-fifth of December and it wasn't a gun or drugs. With Christmas parties, annual leave, and alcohol-related sickness, the opportunity to pull this off were slim to none.

Nash did have some contacts, though, and one who owed her a favour. That person happened to be the DS for the undercover mob and in fairness to this DS, if he could make it happen, he would.

'Get your authorities typed up. I'll provide the backup and arrest team,' Nash said as she got up.

The Silverfox nodded in agreement and left. Despite his hesitance he was a grafter, and knowing he had a team willing to take the job on was half the battle; the rest was getting a UCO to facilitate the buy at such short notice.

Nash picked up the phone to make a call. It was answered after five rings by a gruff-sounding male voice. A voice Nash recognised as that of DS Carl Harris.

'Yeah,' Harris replied, succinct and to the point. It was the type of reply that told Nash she didn't have long to convince him to stay on the line.

'Carl, it's Pip Nash. You awake?'

'Well, I fuckin' am now. What do you want at this ungodly hour of the morning?'

'Ungodly? It's eight thirty. Some of us have been at work three hours already,' she replied.

'Fuck off, Pip. Chances of you being at work in the early hours are a joke. I'll have you know, just as you were sauntering in to start work, I was getting back after an all-nighter,' Harris said with a jovial note to his voice.

'Well you missed a made offensive weapon in the guise of a knife and I know where it is,' Nash retorted as she let that hang. She could hear movement like Harris was getting up.

'You do know it's my office lunch today?' Harris said.

'Every day's an office lunch with you. Look, this will be a quick hit, straightforward, buy bust.'

'Oh, get you! We don't do that anymore, Pip. You'd know that if you agreed to come out and play now and then.' Harris laughed.

'My days of that are done. Way too much work here to mess about getting pissed with criminals all day. So, what do you say? Let's at least meet and discuss it. I can be at your office in an hour and the authorities are being typed up as we speak.'

There was a pause at the other end of the line and a loud yawn. Nash held the receiver away from her ear as she expected some other bodily sound to emit from Harris's waking body.

'What's the urgency? I don't get requests to buy knives and you of all people should know that. They're ten a penny out there so what's so special about this one that you want to go to this degree of subterfuge and expense to get it back?' he asked.

Nash breathed in deeply and explained the situation.

'So there's a possibility this has been used in two murders?'

'Yes.'

'Don't be late. Bring that sly sod from the source unit with you, too. I'll have a few questions for him. A handcrafted made offensive weapon, my arse,' Harris said. The line went dead.

'Grab your stuff,' Nash said to Moretti. 'We're off to meet Carl. We need to grab the Silverfox on our way.'

CHAPTER TWENTY-SIX

The UCO office stank of a heady mixture of various colognes, stale cigarettes, and alcohol. Not too dissimilar to a nightclub toilet, Nash thought as they entered. Nash held her neck scarf up to her face as Carl Harris met them. He'd clearly dressed in a hurry as his slicked-back Afro hair was wet and tied off at the back. He wore an open neck shirt and bling that Puff Daddy would kill for. Nash admired Harris. She'd worked a few jobs with him back in the day and they'd made a good undercover duo.

They'd spent many an evening acting to the best of their abilities and had fun in the process. Harris was a dying breed. Not many lasted the time in the role he had. He was only forty-five but looked years younger. He had great skin and worked out but not to the extent he was overly built. He carried his six-three frame well and made for an imposing adversary when he was in role. Out of role he was a humble man with tenacity for work.

Introductions over, the meeting commenced. The Silverfox stated what he was prepared to reveal, which was everything he'd told Nash, bar the true ID of the informant.

Harris had decided he was the best man for the job.

'So, just to be a hundred per cent certain, your middleman is prepared to meet a black guy and sell to him?' Harris asked as it was important to him. He'd suffered racism his entire life and wasn't about to waste his time with some street punk or knife supplier who'd take one look at him and, from his own ignorance and warped mind, walk away. His time and attention were precious and not to be wasted.

'Yes,' the Silverfox replied.

'You've asked him then?'

'As soon as DI Nash said it was you doing the buy, I put the call in and our friendly did the same his end and confirmed that the seller has no gang affiliation so black, white, pink, or blue he doesn't care, as long as the money is green,' the Silverfox reiterated.

'Good. How much is he looking for?' Harris responded.

'The price is negotiable but bring at least five hundred – cash, obviously,' the Silverfox replied.

'OK, well it's not my preferred way of working and you, Pip, will have to make a decision about when you take the fella out. I'll get the cash authorised and the car I'll be in sorted too. I'll let you know what car so you can spot me when I turn up,' Harris said as he turned to the handler.

'I'll need your man to call the guy and tell him to meet me later at a location I decide. Tell him to bring the knife; I'm not moving all over London chasing it. No fucking about today, as I need to make the lunch. We pay up front for the meal and exclusive use of the venue and bar. It's not cheap,' Harris addressed this specifically to the Silverfox who saluted with two fingers side-on from his forehead.

He and Harris were good. The handler knew the score if anything he'd said wasn't as it was. He wouldn't put an officer on offer. Thankfully the Silverfox was experienced enough to know you didn't lie or piss about when you were putting a colleague in a dangerous position.

Meeting over, the three of them left Harris and went to the canteen. It was thankfully quiet, and Nash got the drinks in as they sat down and planned the rest of the day. The Silverfox had made his own way to the UC office, as he wasn't going to be seen in any police vehicle even if it was unmarked. A good villain will always know Old Bill.

* * *

Nash had an arrest team on standby. She'd decided to arrest the seller as soon as the transaction was complete and when it was safe to do so.

Letting him leave at the point of sale was a high-risk operational move. They could lose him and if he had a gun as backup, then he could start firing as he was in motion. He was equally aware that the firearms controller would prefer this approach rather than having a moving vehicle to deal with.

She'd spoken to the tactical advisor for the firearms team and they'd agreed to support her as far as was considered safe. Nash knew that without armed support, the operation couldn't be done. Harris's safety bothered her, but she was comforted that she had done all she could to ensure the risks were being managed.

They waited thirty minutes until Harris appeared. His eyes searched the canteen until they clocked Nash. He sauntered over with a docket.

'Fuck me, things can happen quickly here on occasions. Especially when the higher-ups have places they need to be, and the Commissioner has an initiative against knife-enabled crime. We're good to go. Have you spoken to your man?' Harris looked at the Silverfox.

'Yes. He won't meet in the car park where you suggested, though. It was too quiet for him. He wants to meet at Brent Cross shopping centre where it's more public. From what I've been told he fears a robbery and wants the insurance of people about. If you agree to the venue the seller will bring the knife to the plot. Then it's down to you to broker the deal as you wish,' the Silverfox replied, smugly satisfied that he'd achieved so much at this time of year.

Harris looked at Nash.

'I had a plan B should the guy not agree and that covered a public place. If you're happy then I'm happy to continue,' she said.

'What are we waiting for then? I'm always up for a challenge and we've come too far to pull the job now. As long as the firearms team are happy then so am I. I know Brent Cross very well, so I don't need to check it out. Drink up and let's get this shit show done,' Harris said.

They rose from the table and left.

* * *

Nash and Moretti left the Silverfox with a colleague who'd arrived at the office. They'd see no more of the handlers until tomorrow. They wouldn't be anywhere near the action as it wasn't their territory. Covert meant just that. They'd be in touch by phone should there be any problem. Nash had phoned and briefed the Intel DS who had organised the outside arrest team. Once the suspect was detained then they'd move in and arrest. The firearms team leader wasn't happy with the venue change but was satisfied they'd have enough time to recce the new venue and assess their tactics. They too had worked that place before, so it wasn't new to them either in terms of tactics. One advantage being it would be busy so the chances of a quick exit by car were slim and the suspect could be contained quickly once the weapon was in the UC's car. If the suspect produced another then they had the skill and training to neutralise that threat.

All would be in plain clothes around the vicinity of the meeting with uniform support in a removal van in the background. Once the strike was announced, and it was safe to do so, the rear doors would open, and they'd deploy and deal with the public. A risk assessment would be completed and if everyone was still happy, the meeting would take place at three o'clock in the car park at Brent Cross shopping centre.

* * *

'How much longer?' asked Moretti as he checked his watch and looked at Nash. He had his feet up on the rear seat of the observation van and stared out the one-way window. DC Jones operated the DSLR camera and took some test shots to ensure he was in focus.

'We're on,' the radio announced as DS Carl Harris's midnight black Nissan Navara cruised into the car park. Harris positioned it into a space away from the shoppers' vehicles. He parked close towards the tree verge but far enough out that he could open the boot.

Moretti scratched his skull as they observed from the rear of the van which had a clear and unobstructed view of Harris's vehicle. Nash wondered when the van was last fumigated as she'd been itching from the moment she'd got inside.

Harris dropped the internal visor and gave himself the once over in the vanity mirror. At the same time he conducted a radio check, and he was clear to the controller of the surveillance team who confirmed this to other units that included Nash. Now they'd wait for the target to arrive and the transaction to go ahead. Nash slowly sat back getting as comfy as she could, mindful not to rock the van and alert outsiders to any occupancy.

They didn't have to wait long for the action to commence. A dark blue BMW 3 Series slowly cruised into view. Jonesy snapped away on the camera. From her binoculars Nash could see two white males, one late thirties, the other mid-twenties.

The younger of the two looked to her the informant type. Unkempt long hair, peaked baseball hat pulled down over his eyes, and looked shifty. She'd dealt with informants and was going on stereotype. The driver was more self-assured. He wore dark shades, had short-cropped dark hair, and a blue Ralph Lauren polo shirt. He had the appearance of someone who was here to shop. Nash moved the binoculars in the direction of DS Harris's car. She could see him, his phone at his ear in conversation while he looked in the vanity mirror.

At the same time, the scruffier looking of the two in the BMW was on his phone. Harris started to talk out the corner of his mouth as he cupped the handset. Nash placed her hand over the earpiece attached to the body-worn police radio in order to hear.

'We're on,' she told the other two. Not that they needed confirmation as they had visual and as far as they were concerned, detective instinct told them these were the two they were looking for. That and a call from Harris told them the suspect's vehicle they should look out for when he got to the venue. He'd asked that himself as he needed to know what car to look for should he be late for any reason. That was his excuse anyway and they bought it. The BMW parked alongside Harris's car. There was no movement from any of the occupants. Harris remained talking on the phone with the passenger still on his. It was a tense time and everyone in the OP van remained alert and on the ball. Nash had insisted on being in the van keeping observation. She knew the signal she'd be waiting for from Harris and insisted on being the one to make the shout to strike. Her murders. Her way. Once she called it, the firearms leader would take over control of the operation.

The passenger door to the BMW opened and the scruffy guy looked around as he stepped out of his car. He moved to the rear of Harris's Navara and got in the back seat.

Nash guessed Harris had arranged this as it all looked natural.

Harris turned down the car radio as he adjusted the rear-view mirror to observe his visitor. A guy who now added a unique odour to the car's interior.

'So, what's up?' Harris asked.

'You know what's up, right?' the guy asked, one hand on the door handle as he avoided eye contact.

'Look, pal, have you got something for me or not?' Harris directed to the side of the face in his vanity mirror. He had a tone that told the man in the back he wouldn't be hanging about on a false promise. He kept the conversation loose and non-committal as to what he had come for. He'd been told on the phone it was a quality handcrafted blade, cutting edge honed to precision, but you could never be certain what was being brought for sale until it was seen.

'It's here. He wants to see the money first then I'll stick it in the boot of your motor,' came the reply from the ferret-faced fella in the back.

'I'll count the cash out in front of you. After that you go get the parcel and bring it back in here for me to look at. After all, I need to see what I'm buying ain't fake or the bag ain't empty. Once I'm happy, the cash is yours to take,' Harris said.

'Sweet,' the fella replied. He could see the driver through the rear window he'd rolled down and nodded to him. The driver of the BMW got on his phone. As he did, the window went up, and the ferret-faced one held his iPhone on FaceTime over Harris's hands as Harris, slowly and methodically, counted out the money.

The count was over. Nash viewed the moneyman via the binoculars as he leaned back and spoke into his phone. In the BMW, the driver nodded as though in agreement with the conversation taking place. The driver hung up and the boot of the BMW was released. Ferret face slid out the back and went to the boot of the BMW. He lifted out a black canvas holdall. He shifted it onto his shoulder and got back into the rear seat of Harris's Navara. She'd missed Harris exiting his side and getting in the back. She focussed the binoculars towards the crevice in the central console and watched as Harris opened the bag and peered inside. He produced a hanky from his pocket and moved the contents of the bag as Nash could see his hand disappear and the outside of the canvas shift.

Jonesy had a chuckle to himself as he clicked away on the camera's shutter. 'Like shooting fish in a barrel,' he said as he concentrated on his breathing, keeping his hands steady as he depressed the shutter button.

Nash saw a shake of hands between Harris and the ferret-faced one. Then the two rear doors opened.

'C'mon, c'mon,' Nash whispered as she continued to view the theatre in front of her.

Harris got back in the driver's seat and produced a plain baseball cap from the glove box and placed it on his head. He engaged the engine. The passenger of the BMW dropped a carrier bag that contained the money in the driver's lap as they both smiled at a job well done.

Harris waited as the BMW moved off and, once he was satisfied they were clear of him, he started towards the rear of the car park in the opposite direction.

'We're on. That's the signal from Harris. If the cap fits take them down!' Nash announced to Moretti and Jonesy as Jonesy watched the BMW moving off. Nash got on the radio. 'Firearms Silver, it's all yours,' she said.

'All received. Silver out,' she replied.

The hustle and carnage of the Christmas shoppers' outings exploded in a series of shouts to *'Get down'* as plain-clothes armed cops appeared from various vehicles, littered about the car park.

Chequered caps were visible on heads as MP5s pointed at the occupants of the BMW. The driver, eyes wide, realised it was all over. The driver's side window was shattered as an armed officer caved the window in. At the same time another officer did the passenger's.

A cop screamed at them, 'Stay where you are, keep your hands where I can see them and don't move.' The MP5 assault rifle levelled at the driver's chest. The screaming was necessary, to be heard over the shouts from the public who were all desperately trying to avoid being caught up in the fracas.

The BMW's doors were opened by other armed cops as both suspects were dragged out to the ground and cuffed. The driver shouted his innocence, telling whoever would listen they had the wrong person.

While this was happening, Harris had pulled over some distance away from the foray and well out of sight. He flicked his hands-free on in the Navara. There was a brief wait then a response at the other end of the line. Harris spoke.

'Yo, Hugo, it's Carl. Job's done. I'll be at the venue in an hour. I'll have the prawn bhuna, pilau rice, and a handful of naan, oh, and a Kingfisher to wash it down, no, make that three it's been a busy morning and I've got a thirst on,' he said as he awaited confirmation of his order then disconnected.

Nash remained in the rear of the van, quietly satisfied as she'd seen the suspects on the ground. The driver still proclaimed mistaken identity. Yawping about a set-up by the police. The passenger remained subdued as he was lifted up following a body search and placed in the back of a vehicle.

'Jonesy, get on to Steve at the office and tell him to come and get us back to base,' Nash requested as they all relaxed and took five. They knew they'd need this brief respite as they'd been on duty for nearly ten hours and now the arrest had been made and the knife recovered, the laborious work of dealing with the prisoner was just starting.

CHAPTER TWENTY-SEVEN

'This interview is being recorded and may be used in evidence if this case is brought to trial. I'm DI Nash, Homicide and Serious Crime Command. The other officer present, is…'

'DS Moretti, same unit.'

'We're in the taped interview room at Holborn Police Station and for the benefit of the recording please give me your full name?'

Nash remained leant forward on the desk that separated them from Dean Kendrick. Kendrick was wearing a police issue tracksuit adorned with blue fluff from the blanket in his cell.

'You know my name already. Dean Kendrick. Bit over the top to have a DI interviewing, ain't it?'

'We're short-staffed,' Nash responded before continuing. 'Is it correct you've agreed to be interviewed without a legal representative, Dean?'

'Yes. I don't need one. I'm prepared to tell you what you want.'

'Well, if you change your mind at any time during the interview, the recording will stop, and one can be arranged for consultation by phone or at the station. Do you understand?'

'Yes.'

'Before I continue with any questions, I must remind you that you are not obliged to say anything, but anything you do say may be given in evidence in court if this case is brought to trial. If you fail to mention something which you later rely on in court, an inference may be drawn from that. Do you understand the caution you've just been given?'

'Fully. I'm not thick.'

Nash having heard the response decided to explain the meaning of the caution anyway. It wasn't out of malice. She treated all suspects the same way and it shut that door from the defence should they wish to claim their client didn't understand what was being said despite them stating they did. Nash gave the date and time and started questioning.

'Dean, it's all right if I call you that?'

'It's my name.'

'Dean, you were arrested today in possession of five hundred pounds cash that you claim wasn't your money?'

'That's right. As I told the lump who dragged me out of my car at gunpoint and slammed me to the ground, I took the fella who was with me to meet a guy as he had some business at Brent Cross. I was headed there to do some Christmas shopping so didn't mind. Season of goodwill an' all that. I'd picked him up at Edgware as he was thumbing a lift. It's Christmas; I took pity on him. Next thing I know I'm being dragged out my motor and I'm here. The cash is his; not mine. You're talkin' to the wrong man.'

Nash paused to see if Kendrick would continue but he sat back and smiled, hands in the air in a gesture internationally recognised as, are we done?

'Well how unfortunate for you, a Good Samaritan, that you got tucked up like that?' Moretti added as he too leant forward mirroring Nash's body language.

'Well, Dean, you can carry on and waste police time by sticking to that story or you can tell us the truth as to why you were there? I will remind you again that if you wish to speak to a solicitor, you can. I recommend you consider what I've said before your next reply,' Nash said as she sat back.

Kendrick looked at the ceiling then back at the two of them. He knew they had more up their sleeves than they were letting on. This wasn't his first time in custody or in a police interview. The last time he'd been arrested was for GBH and he'd got off. This time, his gut was telling him he wouldn't be as lucky.

'OK, OK. If I tell you the truth what can you do for me? I mean, I don't wanna go down for this... this misunderstanding?' he pleaded as he leaned towards them.

'Just get it off your chest, Dean, and then we can see what we can do. I'm in no position to offer anything right now and wouldn't wish to give any false promises,' Nash said.

'Look, the fella I was with told me that another fella he knew was interested in an item of property.'

'What property?' Nash pressed.

'Does that matter?'

'Yes,' Moretti and Nash replied in unison.

'OK, OK, it was a watch, a Rolex, to be precise. The guy who got nicked with me said someone was interested. He set up a meet. I was selling the watch as I needed the cash. He said he knew someone who would want it and called another fella who bought it and drove off before you lot turned up,' he replied as Nash and Moretti looked at each other.

Nash nodded. 'Are you having a laugh?' she said.

'What? No! Straight up. I would've sold it in the shopping centre at a jewellers I know but took his offer instead,' he said. His eyes darted between Moretti and Nash as he sought confirmation one of them was buying his bullshit. His brain told him different.

'So, the guy who you say bought this *watch*, just drove off before you were arrested?' Moretti asked.

'Yeah, just fucked off. Then you lot turned up. Well, not you two but cops, lots of cops.'

'Lots of cops with guns who shouted, "Armed police," I believe. That's according to the arresting officer's notes,' Nash said as she examined a statement. 'Not good enough, Dean.'

Moretti remained silent. The only sound in the room coming from the fluorescent tube as it gave out a low hum and flickered every now and then in a desperate attempt to cling to life.

Dean managed a sip from the now lukewarm cup of tea and gave a long sigh.

'You lot just don't believe anyone, do ya?' Dean mooted. He paused and reached for the Styrofoam cup then realised it was empty. The stress of the situation getting to him as he'd just picked it up moments before. 'Any chance of another tea?' He held the empty cup out like a beggar seeking spare change.

'No,' Nash said.

'That's out of order; withholding drinks!' Kendrick bellowed as spittle covered the desk and Moretti's blue book.

'Call it what you wish. I don't know about you, but I think this initial interview's done?' Nash turned to Moretti who nodded in agreement and motioned to turn the recording off.

'This interview is terminated at–'

'Whoa! Don't touch the fuckin' machine; I need to be out of here and quick. The guy's name is Gary. Well, that's what he told me. Like I said, I'd never met the guy before, but I picked him up today and sold him a Rolex. Before I got nicked, he'd said he'd send someone he trusted to broker the deal, and that's how I met matey boy who was in the car with me. He then said he never had the cash but the man who did wanted to link up and do the deal quick. I'd sent the guy I was with some images and he liked what he saw, so as long as what was delivered was the same, then it was game on. That's how I came across the cash. Now are we done?' Kendrick said and hoped he was.

Nash stared at Kendrick who glanced at her. A stare that had silenced many a man. Kendrick sat back and picked at the top of the empty cup. In his head he hoped this was the final push. The final attempt at nailing him before he was banged up for the night then bailed. Charges quashed by the lack of any evidence as they wouldn't be able to obtain any. He'd agreed with ferret face what story they'd stick to if they were nicked. A story they'd rehearsed. However, like all things in life, much doesn't go to plan.

Nash bent down and took out a blank manila envelope from which she produced a series of images. She displayed them out on the desk like a triptych. Kendrick's Adam's apple bobbed like a boxer in a fight going nowhere but knockout.

'Big bag for such a small watch, wouldn't you say, Dean?' Nash stated as she pointed at the photo of the bag.

'Heavy too, by the way it sagged?' Moretti said.

The cup Kendrick picked at disintegrated on impact as his fist smashed down on it. Neither Moretti nor Nash flinched. They'd seen it coming.

'I'll need that solicitor and a cup of tea.'

CHAPTER TWENTY-EIGHT

Moretti and Nash sat in his job car as they waited on the armed entry team to effect yet another raid. A raid initiated by Dean Kendrick's wise decision to listen to his solicitor's advice, following full disclosure prior to re-interview. The advice was to tell them all he knew, which proved to be a lot. Kendrick had stated that he'd met the person selling the knife and he'd been concerned – his words – following the news of the two, 'sliced to death' – as he put it – that the blade was too hot for him and he wanted rid of it.

Nash could see the way his expression changed from bolshie to a deeper reflective mood when he described where he'd met the suspect with no name to buy the knife. It was the house they were now waiting to storm. A house split into bedsits with the accommodation where the meeting had taken place being on the third of three floors. No risks were being taken here and part of the assessment was to attack it in the early hours as that provided the armed entry team with an element of surprise and control. A police sniper covered the window that overlooked the garden and a dog unit was on standby should anyone, not posing an immediate threat with a knife or firearm, drop and run.

As well as being the keenest Landshark in the dog unit, Thor was also a fast runner and wouldn't hesitate if instructed to act. Thor's bite was legendary and many a handler prayed he would hang on to the sleeve during training as the thought of him letting go and taking another strike at spare flesh wasn't relished.

Nash activated the torch on her phone and brought out the decision log she'd been keeping since the inception of the investigation. This wasn't the first logbook, such was the volume of thoughts that had sprung up in her head during the enquiry, so far.

'Another log entry? Your mind's been on overtime,' Moretti said as he bit into an apple, the juice from which caught Nash's current page.

She wiped it off and continued to scribe. The glide of the Montblanc nib reassured her with each stroke. Once she'd dumped the thoughts from her mind onto paper, she could fully focus on tonight's task.

'It helps me, Nick. You should use one too, it may help you,' she said.

'Nah, why duplicate two great minds?' he replied with a grin.

Their conversation was broken by the sound of the radio and the tactical advisor for the firearms team. All call signs responded with an affirmative as to readiness and she gave the shout. Yet again, a street's tranquil state erupted like Vesuvius.

Within seconds the officers were up the stairs and at the bedsit's door.

They all operated as one slick team. Everyone was where they should be within seconds. The door went through on the observed three count and the armed team entered. A blast of music echoed off the tiny room from two huge floor speakers; Lemmy's voice screamed, 'The ace of spades,' on a volume that shook the walls and caused the first officer to pause in shock but then quickly regain their composure.

One officer went to turn the music down, but the team leader grabbed his arm. Once they'd assessed the room was clear he would be allowed to pull the cord from the wall to stop the music.

CHAPTER TWENTY-NINE

The armed team stood as one in the single occupancy room. They removed their helmets and observed the walls. Walls that were a decoupage of death. One officer began to heave, and he moved to the window, flung it open, and took in some air.

'You need to get up here,' the Tac Advisor said over the radio to Nash, who acknowledged the radio contact.

By the time Nash and Moretti were at the top of the stairs the armed team was outside the room. An officer covered the door. Nash and Moretti suited up and entered.

'Holy shit.' The only words Nash could find to describe what they saw and smelt. Colour and black and white images on the walls depicted death, both human and animal.

Images, everywhere, of open wounds, bodies hanging, people being stoned, shootings, knife attacks, machete wounds, axe wounds, they were all here. A jar containing a mass of red flesh that looked like a tongue. Separate jars that contained single sets of eyeballs, suspended in fluid, adorned the fireplace mantel. A curtain that separated the sleeping section was pulled back, the Tac Advisor confirmed it was moved by police and had been drawn over when they'd entered. The reason being that behind the curtain was a message written in red across the back wall.

Too Late

Below that was a Banksy style stencil of a joker his mouth wide open, eyes pinched shut. Nash suspected blood was used as the writing material of choice. But that wasn't all. A severed pig's head sat in a sink below a mirror, the stench from which had made an officer from the entry team seek fresh air.

Moretti felt a vibration and his hand went to his right pocket. He unzipped the suit, reached in, and retrieved his phone. Another call from a withheld number showed on his screen. Nash was still engrossed in the images on the wall as Moretti answered the call. He was thinking it was the SOCO; he was to be disappointed.

'So, you found my training wall? Well done, Mr Moretti, well done. I hope you enjoyed the music too, a live recording, I believe.' Moretti listened to the same distorted voice he'd heard before.

'I can help you, you just need to meet me, and we can talk. There's no need to keep going down this path, no need at all,' he said.

'Hahahahaha! You think I'm killing to get your attention? You deluded fool. I enjoy the kill. Actually, that's a lie. I enjoy the stalk. The kill is just a necessary evil. A final release of pent-up energy. Did you see my message? Now that *is* for you. It's too late for us all but especially for you, Nick. The pig's head was a step too far, even for me, but I needed the eyes you see… anyway, I'll be seeing you soon, Moretti, very soon.' The voice stopped and the call ended.

'Wait, don't hang up!' Moretti held the phone away from his ear while he spoke into the air. The screen displayed the call's duration. He let the phone drop by his side, still clutched in his hand as he looked up to the ceiling. A ceiling that, he now realised, was covered with ace of spades playing cards.

He felt someone close by and looked down as Nash touched his elbow.

'Who was that, Nick? What's going on?' she asked, as their eyes met above the nose line of the forensic face shields. Moretti knew his time was up. He couldn't contain the information any longer.

'I've had two calls from our suspect. Well, someone who claims to be our suspect and who knows we're in this bedsit,' Moretti said as his gaze settled on Nash. Nash turned away for a beat then back at Moretti.

'And you didn't mention this to me, because…?' Nash pressed.

Moretti blinked and Nash knew she'd hit a nerve as he averted his gaze and turned towards the open window.

'Because I didn't. Because I was told I couldn't. He told… the voice told me not to tell anyone or there would be more death,' he said. His eyes transfixed by the walls as he gripped his phone as though it were his own heart that had escaped.

'You expect me, as your DI, to just take that on the chin? A major investigative line in this enquiry? Fucking hell, Nick!' Nash shouted, hands on hips, eyes ablaze with anger. Angered at his lack of faith, honesty, trust, and confidence.

'You stupid bastard.' Was all she could muster as she walked out of the bedsit taking off her forensic suit as she left.

Moretti said nothing. There was nothing more to be said. He'd fucked up. Again. He should've taken her into his confidence. She was his DI, the lead investigating officer of the enquiry team. But he hadn't. He hadn't because he believed with complete honesty the threat made on the first call. The fact that the suspect had been able to reach him on a number that wasn't public knowledge had troubled him since the first call and he'd started to suspect everyone he was in close contact with.

* * *

Nash had contacted the staff required at the scene: the usual officers for house-to-house and CCTV. Despite the lack of a body it was still a crime scene. She returned to Moretti after she'd had time to compose herself.

'I'm sorry. At least I think I am. I overreacted without considering how you must have felt being put in the position this person has put you in. This is manageable, Nick. Everything is if we share all that we know and don't keep things to ourselves. Now, because of the control this person feels they has over us, or you, in particular, I propose we do nothing different at this time. Make them believe I'm unaware and you've stuck to the protocol. Whatever you do don't lose that phone, and we're going to need to get a line on it to ascertain where the call's being made from. In the meantime log every call they make and exactly what's said. I'd love to take you off the enquiry for your own welfare but I won't. I'm afraid you're the bait with which we can lure this scum out with,' she said as she tentatively touched his arm.

Moretti nodded his head in recognition.

She'd reacted badly in her mind and she regretted it even though Moretti had been out of order keeping a key line of enquiry back, and in the hope of what? That she'd never find out? That somehow it would all go away?

* * *

Nash had got Jonesy to run her back to the office where she'd carried on with her work and ensured the inside team were up to speed on what had been discovered at the address.

It wasn't long before one of the DCs, Adam, approached her with a research docket and a smile that spoke volumes.

'Take a look at this.' He stepped into her office and handed her the docket as though it were gold and she invited him to sit down as she read.

'I spoke with Charlotte, the psych bird–'

Nash cut him short as she looked up from the docket.

'She's a behavioural psychologist with a doctorate in forensic science: Dr Miller to you, not "some psych bird," Adam.'

Adam's face flushed as he made like a goldfish. Nash's expression fused in fury that let him know she had no time for his sexist shit. Shit she'd taken her entire service but had her fill of for one day.

'Sorry, boss. Stupid of me to say,' Adam replied. A response Nash could tell was heartfelt and genuine.

'Carry on,' she said.

The DC continued.

'As I was saying, I spoke with Dr Miller and she requested a chart of known offenders and non-offenders associated with knives and or serious violence. She set a parameter for the search within a mile of the different kill sites. There were surprisingly few people in the system.

But you'd also tasked me to research all former employees from the estate agents who would have had access to the premises. I checked and came up with this guy, Mark Donovan. He didn't have any of the background Dr Miller mentioned. Nick had asked about clubs, too, any that had a fascination with guns, knives and hunting, so I dug about and found that Mark Donovan is a member of a martial arts group who appreciate close-quarter combat and use training weapons to practise. They meet on the first Monday of the month in North London. You can access the club's gallery through their website and see what weapons they use to work with: swords, knives, sticks and nunchaku are the main choice,' Adam said jubilantly.

'That's great, Adam, but being a member of a martial arts club doesn't make him a killer. I should know. Does he have previous? If so, is any of it for violence towards animals or humans? Is he linked to any religious order or faith group? It's good work, I'll give you that, and it's another link with the agency,' came her reply as she put the docket on her desk and smiled in a way that told Adam the meeting was over.

He got up and left her to what she'd been concentrating on before he'd arrived.

He tried to contact Moretti to let him know too but there was no reply.

As far as he was concerned, he'd done his job; he'd passed the information up the chain of command.

Nash was about to continue what she'd been doing when the Silverfox interrupted her. Before he could speak, she shot him down.

'Whatever shit you've dredged up this time, tell Moretti, I'm busy,' she demanded.

'Charming. I've tried his phone, and this is urgent,' he replied with equal voracity.

'Isn't everything urgent with you lot?'

'Yes, but this is properly urgent,' he said, now Nash had calmed down.

She could see from his pale face that he looked out of sorts which was unusual for one of the easiest going cops she knew, aside from Moretti.

'Shut the door,' she said, as she grabbed her drink and offered him a comfy chair. 'So, what's up?'

The Silverfox sat. Nash occupied a chair next to the source handler.

'Look, there's no easy way for me to say this... We've been set up,' he said as he glanced up at Nash. 'Ideally this should come from our controller, you know, DI, to you... but I know he won't say a thing. I'm putting my arse on the line by telling you as this is serious shit.'

'Look, if this is something for your controller, then you should speak to them? I don't operate in your murky world anymore and I'm glad, to be frank. I'm out of that game now so I don't qualify as a replacement sound post for your absent DI,' Nash stated.

The response from the Silverfox wasn't what she'd expected.

'In all my years I've never met a DI who can, at times, be as obtuse and hard-faced as you! I've been in this job way longer than you and dealt with some pretty shitty people, but you... you take the piss, let me tell you. I wish I'd never come up here!' he said and made to get up.

Nash stopped him. 'OK, OK. Point taken. Maybe, just maybe, today you're right. I've been in a shitty mood and that's down to Moretti and these investigations and not you. I apologise. What's happened? I can't promise I can do anything, but I will listen. I can see you're troubled,' she said, with a genuine warmth the Silverfox appreciated.

She waited as he sat back down, bent forward, his head in his hands. As he looked up, his eyes were red.

'I just took a call from a snout's number, except... except it wasn't him, the informant. It was someone on his phone, voice muffled, distorted... they said something about "being too late" and "This tongue ain't for talking," then the line went dead and now his phone's off.'

He was about to continue when Nash's phone rang, and she motioned with her hand for the Silverfox to stop while she answered.

'DI Nash, homicide.'

'It's the main control room. We've just taken a call from a member of the public about a body being found in a garage. I've called you as there's a sign around his neck saying, "for the attention of DS Moretti" and...'

Nash listened as the operator gave more information and the location of where the victim was to be found.

'Send me the details and have the scene secured by local units,' Nash said as she terminated the call.

'Where did your person live?' she asked the handler.

'Why?' the Silverfox replied.

'That was the control room. They had a call about a body in a garage on the Andover with a sign around his neck asking for DS Moretti.'

'That's got to be my informant, Pip. The one who gave us the knife DS Harris bought, he was never at the buy bust. He's not one of the two who was nicked, but he does... did... live on the Andover.'

Nash got up and moved over to the window; outside, a fresh batch of recruits marched.

'They've no idea the shitstorm they've entered, do they?'

CHAPTER THIRTY

Nash grabbed Jonesy on the way out and made him drive. She needed her hands free to make calls and establish a strategy before she arrived at the scene. She'd left a message for Moretti on his mobile and that had been short and sweet – *call me.*

Her mind turned to the jar she'd seen that held the tongue. She hoped this was from the pig and not the victim. They arrived on the Andover to the usual reception. A crowd of residents had gathered on the landing that ran the length of the garage block and two commercial rubbish containers overflowed with filth.

She saw an open drug exchange between two teenage girls, and she wondered just where policing had gone wrong. She thought she understood all too well how it wouldn't be easy to live on an estate in London. Her own parents had lived on one when Nash was born but they'd applied for a transfer when her father got a job offer in Nottingham. They'd moved prior to Nash's start at nursery so she couldn't remember how it would have been to live on one, she only knew anecdotal chat from her parents. There was no excuse for the display of criminality she'd just witnessed but with no home beat or community officers around it was only to be expected.

A homemade sign scrawled in white paint on an exposed brick wall stated "Don't park here" and that's exactly where Jonesy chose to dump their vehicle, placing the logbook on the dashboard as he dropped the visor to reveal a taped "Homicide" sticker attached.

He'd been a beat cop on this estate as well as a DC before he'd transferred to homicide. A couple of scrotes nodded at him as they leaned against the walkway's wall. Jonesy could only see their upper bodies, but he felt confident with all the uniform in the area that nothing would be dropped from above today. Their interest focussed on what was within the dark recesses of garage thirteen.

Nash approached the officer who'd been first on scene. She'd done a great job and sealed the area down to maintain forensic integrity.

'DI Nash, Homicide and Serious Crime Command. What can you tell me?' she asked.

'Not much, if I'm honest. I was first on scene. Everyone else was otherwise engaged; a person unknown had called it in and said there was a body in the garage. When I arrived, I noticed the door was slightly ajar at the bottom. I put on protective gloves and opened it up and ducked under...' She paused for a moment and looked away from Nash.

Nash waited while the officer gained her composure. 'Take your time. I'm sure what you've seen wasn't pleasant and if it's any consolation, it took guts to take a call like this, so don't beat yourself up,' Nash said.

The officer smiled and continued, 'I shone my torch and that's when I saw him; well, you can't miss him really, he's smack in the middle just... just... hanging there with a sign round his neck that said "Call DS Moretti"... blood everywhere round his mouth. A mouth that's propped open by a lump of polished dark rock, or glass. I didn't touch it or go that close. His tongue's gone. I didn't look for it as I didn't want to spoil the scene and I have my body-worn camera on so you can view what I was seeing from this.'

Nash gave her a moment and made some notes. The officer had obviously been an attentive listener at training as the path she'd taken in the garage was appropriate as was the use of the body-worn camera. An advance in technology that not only recorded the officer when they faced a confrontation but also what actions they took on entering a crime scene.

The door for number thirteen had been closed back to where it should be, and Nash understood this was to shield the scene from view. A plastic sheet was being sought to provide further security. Nash turned at the sound of an engine as the SOCO's van arrived. With her was Moretti.

They strode over to outside the inner cordon where Nash and Jonesy stood. Both appeared exhausted and Nash could see Moretti had changed clothes. He always carried another set in his grab bag, even if it was just a T-shirt and jeans.

'So here you are. I wondered where you'd got to, Pip. Thanks for organising the cavalry at the last place. I needed it. I understand a mouth is missing a tongue here? Well, we may have found that in a pickling jar at the other address,' Moretti said as he surveyed his surroundings.

'Jonesy, contact the office and get a couple more up here and start knocking on doors,' Nash said. She turned back to Moretti and the SOCO who were both getting suited up.

There would be no further conversation between Nash and Moretti about his mystery caller until this scene was complete. They had to focus and getting distracted by their fallout wouldn't help this victim.

'Right, let's get to work, shall we?' said the SOCO as they followed her into the garage.

CHAPTER THIRTY-ONE

The lack of daylight hours hadn't hampered the investigation. They'd worked diligently and pretty much wrapped things up by the time the natural light faded and the street lamp timers activated. Not that they made much difference to the area – there were so few that worked thanks to the ingenuity of the local dealers who'd smashed the bulbs and ensured their nocturnal criminality remained in the dark where they desired it to be.

Jonesy gathered up the last of the exhibit bags and put them in the boot of the car. He had been instructed to take the exhibits back to base and book them into the storeroom. The SOCO had the samples she required and would deal with those herself.

'So, who wants dropping where? I don't mind a round robin on my way back to the office, it's all overtime now after all,' Jonesy asked.

Moretti looked at Nash to see what plans she had. She'd agreed that all that could be done, for the time, had been.

'I'll get a cab, Jonesy, I'm not far from here,' Nash said.

'Can I share that? I'll carry on from yours to where I need to be,' Moretti asked.

'Sure,' she replied as she got on her phone to look up a local cab firm. As she did, she heard a shout from the balcony above. A male in his mid-fifties with slicked back salt and pepper hair and groomed beard appeared on the balcony above. Nash looked up in the direction of the voice and saw him as he waved at her. 'Fuck,' she muttered to herself. The last thing they needed was to be getting involved in a local borough issue.

'Sir, if you have an issue that requires police, please call your local station. We're not the ones you need,' she said.

The male remained where he was and shook his head in disappointment. 'I don't need your help. I'm a cab driver about to start work and overheard your conversation. I was going to offer to take you or any other officer where they wished out of support, that was all,' he replied as Nash bit her bottom lip.

'That would be so good of you,' she said.

'No problem, love. I'm a registered cabbie. I'll be down in a jiffy and will wait until you're done,' he said with a wave as he left to get his vehicle.

Nash smiled back at him and looked at Moretti who suppressed a laugh. 'What? I suppose you knew he was a cab driver, did you? Not someone who'd just bludgeoned his whole family to death?' she replied, exasperated.

'You need a meal and a break, DI Nash, and I'm going to facilitate that if you'll let me?' Moretti asked, hopeful she'd agree. He too just needed to eat and clear the air with her.

'As long as it's edible and local to me then the answer's yes,' she said as they heard the tone of a horn behind them.

Nash flopped down on the back seat and leant her head against the window as the cab moved off. Moretti sat, legs spread-eagled, with his bag at his feet.

* * *

They'd stopped at a Tesco on the way back to hers and got in the supplies they'd need. Nash paid for everything, including a good tip for the cabbie, then Moretti cooked the food they'd picked up. Food finished, they both sat on cushions on the floor. Nash's flat occupied the top floor of a converted Edwardian house. The rooms were large and airy. She had a bohemian taste in furnishings and loved nothing more than collapsing into a set of large beanbags that adorned the floor space. She didn't own a TV as she had enough bad news during her day without having to endure it again when she got home. She'd had enough of shows about individuals keen to get laid on an island all in the name of fame. She preferred the radio for news and plays.

'I need to update you on some stuff before I forget,' Moretti announced.

'OK, go on. I've something to update you on too, as it goes.'

'So, we lifted some prints at the flat, which may be a start. The SOCO thinks there'll be something from the tape used to fix the pictures to the wall, hopefully DNA from spent skin, so that's also good. The tongue in the jar is human. We'll have to wait and see if it's a match for our last victim. I hope you don't mind but I called the DCI and he's authorised everything as top priority and thrown money at the submissions. He's also phoned the section head and explained the severity of the case. He's been assured it will be dealt with as quickly as possible but with Christmas around the corner it's all excuses about time and no staff.' He paused. Nash didn't say anything and listened. She felt it was the wisest move after the day they'd had.

'The last flat is another from the agency. House-to-house had a result. A resident in a house opposite stated she'd noticed a light on upstairs a few days ago. She'd thought it strange as she'd shopped the letting agents to the council who in turn shut the bedsits down due to health and safety violations. Anyway, she'd called the council again and they said they'd look into it. We got there first and thank God we did. So, what's your news?' Moretti asked.

'That young DC, Adam, from Intel came to see me. He had a docket and was all excited about the prospect that he'd traced the killer...' She paused. Moretti glanced up at her as she continued.

'He'd responded to what you'd tasked at the meeting and had done some good work. He traced a person who had a link to the letting agents and is a member of a martial arts club who concentrate on close combat with weapons,' she said.

Moretti coughed. 'Come again? Why didn't you tell me all this earlier? Isn't this exactly what you'd had a go at me about?'

Nash swallowed and her mind turned over what was in the docket and why she'd taken the decision she had. Maybe she'd been a bit hasty in her dismissal of what Adam had been telling her.

'Look, it sounds better than it is; the only link was that he used to work for the letting agents showing potential renters around when Peterson couldn't be arsed.'

'What was his access to keys like? Did he pick them up? Carry a spare set for each vacant address?' Moretti probed.

'I never got that far,' Nash said as she slumped back against the wall.

Moretti slugged a beer from a bottle. 'You should have told me, Pip, I am your DS and we could have talked it through,' he said as Nash turned towards him.

'Fuck me, that's rich coming from you, that is! The very same DS who didn't tell his DI about a suspect who "apparently" knew our every move as he was in contact with him! Great work, Sherlock!'

They were both up off the floor now. Face-to-face.

'What else is there?' Moretti demanded.

Nash shifted her feet and weighed up whether to let him know, then decided they needed a clean sheet and it wouldn't matter anyway as he needed to be aware. He was her DS and a good one, too, despite his recent behaviour.

'The guy in the garage was the source who gave up the knife Harris bought. The controller on the source unit wanted to keep that fact under wraps but the handler couldn't in all good conscience so he came to me,' she said as they both began to calm down.

The tension in the room dissipated. Moretti sat back down and Nash remained as she was, her head full of the day.

Nash's phone vibrated and she picked it up. There was an email with a heading of Urgent. She swiped the screen and read it in full.

Moretti saw her face and sensed she was reading a message of significance. 'Well?' he said, as he watched Nash look away from her screen and back to him.

Nash swallowed. 'The knife Harris had bought – it's been confirmed as the one used in the two murders. The blade's made from obsidian, a rare volcanic product. When it's crafted into a blade it has a cutting edge far superior to steel. The rock that was found in the mouth of the victim in the garage was of the same product in its pure form,' Nash said. Moretti beamed a smile of joy. Nash felt elated they'd recovered it from the tactics employed, but couldn't help thinking the killer had set her up in some way. That they knew she would try to get an undercover officer to buy the weapon. How? She couldn't answer that.

It also concerned her why this killer had sought Moretti's attention. Why go to such great lengths when they could have found out where he worked and made contact there? Whoever it was clearly knew enough about him: where he worked, what department, even his movements.

The Detective Superintendent was also sending Nash email demands so they could update the media, who were getting sick of the usual platitudes when they knew the bodies were piling up.

Mark Donovan's name had been thrown into the pot and was looking good, but it was still far from clear it was him. Kendrick wouldn't say whom he got the knife off. Point-blank refusal to even say whether it was a man or a woman. His solicitor stated his client had assisted enough. The advice given to Kendrick's accomplice was to make no comment. Both had clearly decided what they were prepared to say or not say, and they'd stuck to it.

Nash contacted Charlotte and she agreed to come to their offices the next day.

Despite the information there was nothing more that could be achieved that evening. It would take planning and an office meeting to address the way forward. Moretti took the underground home. He clung to the pole as the carriage swayed and his mind longed for his holiday. He felt well and truly lost. He'd rather be lost in a tropical paradise than lost in a multiple murder enquiry.

CHAPTER THIRTY-TWO

It was now 9 a.m. and Nash called her team to order. They'd assembled in the briefing room — a sea of red eyes, the men sporting stubble-adorned chins.

'Here's what we have so far: the tongue in the jar from the flat has been matched with the victim from the garage.

This work was expedited by means of a phone call to a known lab technician. A favour owed to our DCI.' Nash paused, and certain eyebrows were raised around the table, but no questions were asked.

'DC Porter is the FLO and he's out with the victim's family as I speak. The knife purchased by DS Carl Harris was made from a volcanic substance called obsidian. Obsidian is a naturally forming volcanic glass with pure obsidian being dark in appearance hence the image we saw on CCTV. I don't wish to go into all the scientific aspects of it here; look it up yourselves if you're interested. It was used in the manufacture of an ancient weapon called a *macuahuitl* which consisted of a wooden handled club with several embedded obsidian blades. The knife we've got here is more like a dagger. It has a wooden handle and a black blade that we've already witnessed is lethal. For those of you who love your vinyl as I do then you may already be aware that obsidian has been used in the manufacture of turntable plates since the 1970s.

'Fingerprints from the bedsit are in the system and so far, there's no match on PNC. Adam has established a possible suspect. A male called Mark Donovan has links to the letting agency that has control over all the properties that have either been a scene or linked to our victims. He also belongs to a martial arts club in North London...' Nash waited while the voices of hope that resonated at this information subsided.

'So where is this Donovan now?' a DC asked.

'We don't know and establishing that is now a main focus of this investigation. Enquiries with the letting agency have ceased as Neil Peterson isn't contactable. All his phones are off, he's also not at his home or office. With the links to all our properties from his agency and the card found at his office, I'm of the opinion he knows more than he's been letting on. I don't believe from having met him that he could be the killer, but he's disappeared now.

He's either done a runner or is laid low with Donovan. We need to try to find them both.'

The name Mark Donovan nagged at Moretti's addled brain. He thought he recognised it, but his head was such a mass of information he struggled to be sure where he'd come across it.

Dr Charlotte Miller was at the briefing and spoke up. 'Our killer would've likely had an adverse childhood experience or an incident of adversity that may have triggered these horrific events. You need to check with social services to see if they hold any records for Mark Donovan and Neil Peterson. If they do, then they may hold details of family or friends they would turn to at a time of crisis,' she said.

Nash nodded her approval at the suggestion and noted George making an entry in his actions book to raise this as a line of enquiry. There weren't many suspects without some adverse history or at least one trigger event that could be traced back to childhood. A last known address had been found for Donovan, but Nash didn't hold out much hope of him being there, not after all the running around. Wherever he was, the police would have to dig deep to establish.

This guy had become used to a nomadic way of life. Sofa surfing wasn't an option with him as he appeared to prefer vacant or condemned properties by what the team were seeing. By all accounts he must have access keys to the units managed by Peterson as there was never forced entry to any of the premises.

Nash turned to the Silverfox. 'I need your sources asking about the location of both Peterson and Donovan. They are a priority for me. I've also liaised with the DI on the Homicide Task Force and his team will react to any information that comes in about these two.'

The handler nodded his understanding. The HTF were a unit dedicated to hunting down those wanted for murder or sought by police in relation to the offence. They had access to covert kit and other methodologies. This was their bread-and-butter work. If anyone could find them, they could.

'We know the club Donovan belonged to. It's a legitimate club, well-respected. The head of the club is an ex-cop and DS Moretti and I will visit him. The more of you I have available for the current enquiries the better. Plus, I wouldn't want you thinking the supervisors weren't willing to do some legwork.'

Laughter sounded as Nash took a sip of coffee. Meeting complete, they all departed to get on with their respective duties.

CHAPTER THIRTY-THREE

Moretti used his warrant card to scrape the ice from the window of his car. The ice wasn't too thick, and the plastic stripped it away with ease. He wiped any excess freeze on his trousers like a barber would strop a razor. He'd slept well and felt refreshed, ready for the long hours he intended to put in. He'd always loved early turns at this hour of the morning. It was 5 a.m., the sun not yet in the sky – the occasional trill of a bird indicated the serenity would soon change as the city came to life. After yesterday's meeting, the team had got on with the day's business. A day of chasing outstanding actions.

Nash had decided to get them away at a reasonable hour as she was conscious of their workload. They were running on empty and needed a rest period, just as a prisoner would be entitled to. With three major enquiries and one team, she could only do what she could do, and she wasn't about to risk her staff's health through excessive hours and no sleep.

Nash had left Moretti a message before she'd turned in, that he should pick her up today and they'd work together. The main area of work concentrated on the manhunt for Mark Donovan and Neil Peterson. Whether either of them had pulled the trigger or not, they still had many questions to answer, one of which was how the tongue of a murder victim came to be in a room they had access to. That alone was enough to make them suspects in anyone's book, along with Peterson's recent absence.

The jar was clean of marks, but she'd expected nothing less. Nash had reflected on her decision-making and in hindsight had been too dismissive of what she was being told by the Intel DC – a rare lapse of judgement she vowed not to repeat.

Moretti had also obtained a recording device and this reassured her. A device he could place on his phone should he get another call from his new friend. He needed to make an attempt at getting the voice recorded just in case the audio lab could clean it up enough. Nash still chose to keep this information between them. Whoever was making the calls was close and she didn't want to risk this getting leaked after the voice had warned of the consequences. She knew too well that if it remained with them then it was safe. No confidential enquiry or meeting was safe in this job.

* * *

Moretti sat in the car as the engine warmed up, and waited until he could see out the windscreen before he set off. He used the time to check the recording kit, which amounted to a suction cup microphone that stuck to the receiver end of the phone should he get a call.

The microphone attached to a digital recorder, a set-up he'd used in the past to record calls he suspected could come back to bite him, but in the end never did. He played back the recording he'd made when Nash had contacted him and got his answering machine. It recorded his request for the caller to leave a message and her voice leaving the details of when he should pick her up. All was in order. He wiped the recording, as he didn't want Nash playing it and thinking he was now recording all their calls. He'd never dream of doing that.

He made good time to Nash's flat. He'd called when he was five minutes away. She waited in her street as he pulled up and the car's headlights swept over her. She was dressed casually in jeans, black boots, a black padded thermal coat with a beanie, and woollen gloves. She got in his car.

Nash blew into her bare hands and messed with the dials on the air vents to direct the warmth from the blower over her legs, which felt frozen.

'I thought you'd got the heating fixed in this heap?' she said as tepid air trickled out the grill.

'Not yet. I made the phone call, but it all sounded long-winded and the car would be off the road for too long, so I never bothered. Besides, I'm normally in yours.'

'So where to, then?' Moretti asked as he wiped the inside of the windscreen with a discarded tissue he'd found in the door pocket.

'I thought we'd get some breakfast then figure out where to go from there. I've a couple of actions I need to chase. I know a good cafe that's open, if you're up for that?' Nash replied, hopeful he'd be in agreement.

'Well that's the first good decision you've made in a while,' he replied.

Nash raked the recline adjuster on her seat. She squirmed her back into a comfy position and closed her eyes.

* * *

They ate well and, while sitting down, Nash had phoned into the office to check everyone was present and occupied. Nash had also spoken to Moretti about the current threat to life he was under as a result of the phone calls. She insisted on giving him an Osman warning letter – a legal requirement resulting from a court ruling in Osman v United Kingdom – that informed him he was at risk of serious harm. He'd looked at it and laughed. As long as he agreed to the management tactics they'd discussed, she said they'd continue as they were. He shrugged it off and placed his copy of the warning in his pocket.

The Homicide Task Force were out at the last known address for Donovan, waiting to see if there were any signs of life from within it before considering the next step.

Nash left it with their DI and DS to decide tactics but on the understanding she wanted him nicked.

The curtains to the flat hadn't moved and no lights had been seen inside. It was a house split into four flats and the one they were interested in was on the ground floor. Nash considered it a wise choice as it would be easy for Donovan to escape from should he need to. The HTF were prepared to wait as it was only 7 a.m. and the suspect could still be asleep or simply not in. What they did know was that the flat wasn't vacant. A covert recce showed a furnished downstairs living room with plates of food on the floor. The bedrooms for all the flats were to the rear and that's where two of the HTF were situated, with a further two officers who kept watch at the front. If anyone left or entered, they would be seen.

Donovan wasn't claiming benefits and the team were waiting on other financial checks to be returned so they could ascertain how he might be getting money. If they could establish a place of employment it would be another lead. He also didn't drive. Nash had an action for all cab firms within a mile's radius of the murder sites to be visited to see if anyone had been picked up or dropped off nearby on the nights in question. She was aware the task was a big one, but phone calls to the firms weren't enough. Nash needed to be certain the right person was spoken to and not some random person who happened to pick up the phone and fob the police off. This was harder when a cop was on the doorstep and wouldn't leave until he or she had the answers they desired.

The suspect would have had to use the holdall the knife was in. Kendrick had confirmed it wasn't his, and that the knife had come in it inside a padded carved wooden box. The box he'd agreed to hand over to police. He'd kept it at first as it was nice, but realised its connection to death so was glad to be rid of it.

Nash needed to find Donovan fast. An arrest would give hope to her frustrated team. The tabloids had headlines like "Christmas Killer Bites Again", despite no evidence of cannibalism. The editor for that particular paper stated nothing was implied by the headline. The bite reference wasn't to be taken literally and they couldn't control what the good members of the public read into it. They then asked for an exclusive to balance the lead story, which was flatly refused.

The media couldn't accept there was no CCTV to publish a still image from or a name with picture to display. One paper threatened to publish an article on police incompetence citing lack of career detectives as the reason for so little movement in the investigation. Nash wasn't unsupportive of this. Despite the spurious nature of the claim, it would highlight an issue that needed to be kept alive in the minds of the public.

They were back in the car now when Moretti's phone vibrated demanding his attention. Attention he didn't wish to give. He looked at the screen and the withheld number, grabbed the suction cup from the recording device and whacked it on the back of the phone as he turned it on, then answered.

'Moretti.'

'Good morning, Moretti. You're up and about bright and early this morning, as is your beautiful boss. Such a joyous combination of brawn and brains. Forgive my call but I have a quick question I hope you'll be able to answer?'

The distorted voice came through loud and clear. Nash moved closer so she could hear what was being said, her face went pale at the sound of the suspect's voice. She felt a slight sense of guilt at how she'd reacted to Moretti as she wondered herself how she'd have dealt with the evil intrusion into her private life.

'I'm in no mood for riddles so make it clear,' Moretti replied. Probably not the best response but he realised the voice was never going to play his game and he just had to listen and respond.

'Touchy, touchy, detective, you should get more sleep. It does wonders for the nervous system. There's no riddle. I'm not The Riddler, that character was make-believe. I just wondered how much longer you were going to remain sat where you are, as I'd hate you to be getting bored on my account? I can always find someone else to keep you busy? All you have to do is say. Really, it would be my pleasure,' the voice said, as the words returned to breath.

Moretti remained still, as did Nash, but the temptation to look around where they were was just too strong. Nash was the first to break as she got out of the vehicle. Moretti remained silent and waited for the suspect to continue, but he didn't.

'Fuck!' Moretti exclaimed as he threw the phone down on the seat and got out to find Nash. She was kerbside sat on a low wall.

'Why'd you get out the car? He's hung up, he must be watching,' Moretti said as he sat beside her.

There were so many places the suspect could observe them from as they'd pulled over off the Holloway Road outside The Floirin pub. The area was busy with vehicle and foot traffic. The location was a mix of both residential and commercial properties. Moretti took his tobacco pouch and pipe from his coat pocket and began to load it up. A silence came over them as they indulged their rituals.

Moretti furiously struck the flint on his Zippo then gave up as it failed to spark. Nash offered a throwaway plastic lighter, which he graciously accepted. She always carried one in case a suspect worth turning desired a light. It's the smallest things that make the biggest difference. He ducked into a doorway to shield the flame as he held it up to the bowl and got a decent blaze going. Nash spoke first now he'd had time to take on some nicotine.

'He's not watching us the way you think,' she said as she watched the traffic pass them by.

'Oh yeah? Why'd you reckon that?' Moretti asked.

'He'd want us to know we were being watched by him. He'd have told you he knew I was out the car. That's why I got out. He's having fun and he wants you to know that. He wants you to know that while you're tearing your hair out trying to locate him, he's having a blast. How he knows we're here I don't understand, but he's not conventionally close,' Nash finished as she ingested a lungful of his smoke.

'Say that last bit again?'

'What part of it?'

'The last sentence, say it again, word for word,' he asked her.

'OK, he's not conventionally close?'

Moretti waved his pipe at her and motioned for her to follow him away from the car towards the Holloway Road. The slow trundle of commuter traffic made conversation trickier, which is what Moretti wanted as he raised his voice slightly and moved closer to Nash.

'He's bugged the fucking car, Pip. You're right, he's not conventionally close because he's tracked my fucking car!'

Nash's eyes widened as she nodded in agreement with Moretti. Moretti took the neck of his pipe out of his mouth as he thought, Nash already one step ahead of him.

'We can't use this car anymore. I need the tech boys to confirm or disprove the theory. I hope to God you're wrong because if you're right, then I've got a serious security breach on my hands, Nick. Whoever it is, is fucking close to us. Close enough to know your car and to have planted a device,' Nash said as Moretti placed the pipe's stem back in his mouth and deliberated on what she'd said.

Nash was pleased he'd moved her away from his car as she knew technology was publicly available that captured both sight and sound. She'd used it herself, so she was paranoid about certain things she discussed within any vehicle.

'I'll get the vehicle sweep organised. It will be done as a confidential enquiry and I suggest we do every car in the fleet, Nick. It might not be just yours; he could have the whole lot bugged,' Nash said. Moretti was in agreement.

'We can't tell the team, Nick. As much as I'd like to, I'm reluctant to include anyone beyond us for the time being. That goes for a sweep of the office too. I can't risk doing that until I know about the fleet. I can manage the cars but doing the offices without raising suspicion is trickier. Let's reassess once we've confirmed if the fleet's wired or not. Send out a directive for all vehicles to be left at base including ours. I'll blag a spare from team three as they're stood down. Any outside enquiry can use theirs. Say it's come from traffic OCU: checking vehicle record data, new damage found, logbook entries, you know what I mean. The HAT car will have to be done, covertly, offsite. Let's get this back to base and dump it. Hopefully they can sweep the car later then I'll decide what to do with it. I'm minded keeping it live if it's bugged. I don't want to alert him,' Nash said.

'Are we certain it's this Donovan, Pip? Let's say it is and there's a device on my car. How in the fuck did he access it? It means he knows where I live or... or...'

'Or he's one of us,' Nash replied.

CHAPTER THIRTY-FOUR

Nash's fear was confirmed. Moretti's vehicle had been discreetly examined under the guise of a mechanic taking it for a couple of hours to repair the defective heating fan. All the team knew it was knackered and didn't question a thing when someone dressed in mechanic's overalls purporting to be an operative from the TSU collected the keys and made Moretti sign a fake release document.

'Have it back with you in a couple of hours, skip. It'll be like the Sahara in there once I've sorted it,' he'd said as he caught the keys Moretti threw for him.

The tracking device itself was small and provided tracking only. No images.

It may have been small but was robust enough to cling to Moretti's vehicle via two powerful magnets and feedback its data via an app to any mobile device or computer. The battery was guaranteed to last six months before it required attention. It was waterproof, rugged, and fit for purpose. From what Nash and Moretti were shown, via a phone picture, it looked better than any device they'd use. The tracking device was taped in position with extra strong tape. This had been forensically examined but not removed. The tape was caked in mud and road dirt. To put anything new in place would draw suspicion if the suspect were to check on his or her work for any reason.

The consensus was that whoever had planted it didn't want to get it back, hence the belt and braces approach with the tape when the magnets were designed to secure it in position without loss of strength. What forensic evidence could be gained from the tape in the state it was in was weak, but Nash insisted on at least trying to capture anything they could, even if that was a soil sample.

As instructed, the device remained live. Nash didn't wish to show her hand yet.

'So, what now?' Moretti asked as Nash closed the door to her office and threw the car keys back on her desk.

'We wait,' she replied as she sat down.

'Wait? What for? Another kill?' Moretti replied, desperation in his voice.

'Look, Nick, we're doing all we can to trace Donovan and Peterson. Unless you've any other ideas then I suggest we go and speak with the martial arts club manager and see if he can shed any light on Donovan,' Nash said.

She took out her car keys and began pressing the fob from Moretti's window to locate it in the car park. The indicator lights flashed, and she was happy.

'Let's go then, Sergeant. Our chariot awaits.'

* * *

They'd decided to meet the manager at the club. The dojo they trained in was situated below ground. It was a well-respected club having been in existence for over seventeen years. Nash had called and enquired about joining and wished to see the facilities first. Her request was accepted as the manager was down there and could see her for ten minutes. Ten minutes was all she required. They needed the manager on side just in case the suspect made contact or appeared at the club. The manager being an ex-cop, they hoped it would be a matter of meet, greet, and he'd be on-board with what they wished to achieve.

They'd decided to get the tube and were soon at the location. Cabs waited in line as commuters and tourists mingled and darted about.

They arrived at the entrance to the club. Moretti buzzed an intercom and waited. After a matter of minutes, it was opened by a male in his late fifties, six foot six in height of a burly muscular build. He wouldn't have looked out of place as a bouncer in an East End pub. He smiled and waved them both in. They followed him towards a small office. The club was quiet as it wasn't in use.

He invited them to be seated and they both sat down. Mr Briggs sat behind a small desk.

'So, we do a competitive rate for couples should you both wish to sign up?' he said as he looked between them.

'That won't be required, Mr Briggs. We're actually police officers here on a different matter,' Nash said as she produced her warrant card. Briggs reached out and examined it and did the same with Moretti's.

'Work for health and safety now, do you? We had an unannounced inspection done last week. So, what can I help you with?' He sounded pissed off as he put away the joining pack that he'd prepared for Nash's arrival. He sat back and stared at Nash.

'I'm sorry for the subterfuge but it was necessary. You're ex job, I understand?' Nash enquired.

'Yes. Officer Safety trainer. So, what's it all about? Your own OST tickets expired and you want a fake one?' Briggs said.

'We're investigating a murder. A name came into the enquiry with links to this club. That's why we're here. We hoped you may be able to assist,' Nash started off.

'Go on?'

'Does the name Mark Donovan mean anything to you?'

'Mark? Yes, yes, of course. He used to train here. He was one of our best fighters at groundwork and close-quarter combat. Why do you need to know? Is he a suspect?'

'A person of interest,' Nash qualified.

'You said he used to train here? Has he left?' Moretti asked.

'He left about three weeks ago, and we haven't seen or heard from him since. Truth is he'd become withdrawn. He'd turn up, train for about twenty minutes, then leave. He used to be quite a sociable guy but recently he wasn't the same. He'd often be seen just sat in his Motörhead tour T-shirt as he listened to music on his headphones from his phone or iPod or what have you. He also pulled out of an upcoming event where he would have been certain to win, as the competition was weak by comparison. But there you go, people change, I guess,' Briggs said as he looked at Moretti with a look of resignation.

'Do you have any photos of him? Or an address we could have?' Nash asked.

'I should do. The address I'm not certain of as he moved about quite a bit but always let us know where he'd be staying,' he said as he began to interrogate his computer.

Nash noticed his furrowed brow as he leant in towards the screen.

'That's odd?' he said after he'd finished waving the mouse about the desk.

'Everything OK?' Nash asked.

'Well, no, actually. We keep computer records of all our people as we log training qualifications and any medical details against the fighter's name, but Mark's file has disappeared. It's not coming up at all and that's where his image would be,' Briggs said as he stared at the screen.

Nash glanced across at Moretti who raised his eyebrows. She thought back to Peterson's computer at the letting office and how the files had been altered there.

'Does Mark have an aptitude for computers, Mr Briggs?' she asked.

Briggs looked up from the screen at the mention of his name.

'Absolutely. He was instrumental in setting up the system here...' Briggs's voice tailed off as the penny dropped and his retired police brain awoke from its slumber.

'Ah, I see where you're going with that, Detective Inspector, I see exactly where you're going and, now, I feel such an idiot at agreeing to let him set the system up.'

'Don't be. How did you know he was capable of this task? You'd have to have a decent knowledge of computers and software?' Nash suggested.

'I didn't think he'd go and wipe files,' Briggs began before Nash cut him off.

'No, I mean why him? Why let him set your system up in the first place and not an outside firm?' she asked with a natural curiosity.

'Money. Mark's a natural on a computer. He'd studied it online and he demonstrated just how he could help. He also agreed to do it in exchange for membership to the facilities. It was a bargain as there was so much work that needed doing,' Briggs said as his voice tailed off in lamentation at his cost-cutting decision.

Moretti had got up and was deep in observation of some of the photos that were displayed on the walls.

'Tell me, if he was such a good fighter, he must have appeared in some publicity photos for the winners? There has to be an image of him somewhere?' Moretti threw out.

'You know, you'd be right in that assumption under normal circumstances, Inspector, but he insisted on not being in any photos at all, aside from his membership one, which was mandatory if he wished to be part of the club. To my knowledge he was so secretive about his identity he didn't have any social media accounts either. We had to either email or phone him if there was a change to the usual club night or a competition. Might I ask what murder this is? There's been so many and, no… not… you're here for the Christmas Killer, aren't you? Of course, you are. The guy that's been going about London with a knife and killed three people? Fuck me, my brain's not what it was since leaving the job all those years ago,' Briggs said as he looked at Nash.

'You're right. We need to find him and fast. Is there anything you can help us with? Anyone here who's a mate of his who may know where he is now? Any phone numbers you may have contacted him on? The email address he was using, anything at all would be good right now,' Nash said as she sat back down.

Briggs rubbed his chin, which was adorned with two-day-old grey stubble that suited him and matched the thick thatch of grey hair he'd managed to keep despite his years.

'Look, I have a number I used to call him on in my phone, you can have that and the email address, too. He would always answer the number I called him on for club meets or lifts to events. Talking about social media and his secretive side, there's something else you may need to know. He was a looked-after child when he was younger. He was removed from his family and placed into care when he was three or four; ever since then he's never had a photo taken that would appear in anything public. He mentioned this to me when he demanded no publicity for his success in events. He didn't want his birth family knowing him; he was ashamed of having been removed despite them being unable or not caring enough to look after him, so he said. I tried to reassure him that as an adult they'd never recognise him, but he just insisted he was used to things being that way and didn't wish to change. He changed his surname to Donovan in recognition of the long-term carers who looked after him until they died. Car accident. About a year ago, I recall. Strange how people can open up to you and he always did when we were in the car on the way to a fight. We'd meet here, grab the gloves and helmets from the kit room and off we'd go. He always insisted on being in the back and would talk and talk.' Briggs paused as he reflected on memories his subconscious fired up.

Moretti and Nash remained silent letting him talk, not filling in the pauses in the hope he would come out with more. He didn't.

'Mr Briggs, did he ever say what his previous surname was?' Nash nudged him after she felt he'd finished thinking.

'Stokes. I'm sure it was Stokes. I do hope you're wrong. He had such amazing potential,' Briggs said, his smile downturned at the mouth.

'Thank you. I think we've taken up enough of your time now so if you could give DS Moretti the telephone number and email address you mentioned, along with all your contact details, we'll leave you alone. If he should get in touch at all then please take this number and call me directly,' Nash said as she handed Briggs a piece of paper with her mobile written down.

Once Moretti had the number from Briggs's phone, they left and headed back to the tube station.

As they walked Moretti began to slow until he came to a stop that caused people behind him to mutter and move around him.

'What's up?' Nash asked.

Moretti moved to the side of the pavement and rested against a wall. He casually observed the people that walked by them before he turned to Nash.

'I know him, Pip,' Moretti said quietly.

'How?' she responded with a caring tone of voice.

'I was the officer that was involved in removing him from his birth family and placed him in care.'

CHAPTER THIRTY-FIVE

The incident room was a hive of activity now the new information had been fed in. The number given by Briggs was still live and an application to the Home Secretary for intrusive surveillance was underway. Nash needed that phone hooked up and fast along with Moretti's work phone as she felt a strong responsibility towards his safety. If the killer dropped his phone but still contacted Moretti then it would help her investigation. She decided to not let Moretti know that his work phone would be listened to. Not out of any concern of wrongdoing on his part, just that she wanted him to remain natural when called.

Social Services were being visited, as well as Donovan's, or Stokes's, previous social workers being traced. The HTF had reported no movement at the property. Nash felt confident they could now locate him. She'd had an All Ports message issued that placed all ferries, Eurostar and airports on alert. Not that there was any intelligence Mark intended to leave the country but nevertheless, Nash didn't want to be caught off guard.

The first piece of positive news came in earlier than expected. The warrant for intrusive surveillance had been granted at the same time cell site analysis pinpointed the phone's signal – right where the HTF were in position.

'He must be laying low or he's devised another way in and out of the building. I once had a suspect who used a loft's crawl space between terraced houses to exit an area. Cunning sod he was,' Nash remarked as they got back in her vehicle and started towards the tiger trap gate.

Once they were clear Nash activated the two tones and lights in the covert car and they were away over to the address where the HTF were already watching, waiting to pounce.

Nash blipped the accelerator and Moretti reached and grabbed the handle above the passenger door window. It wasn't that Nash couldn't drive safely; she could. It was the others who didn't get out of the way quick enough that were the issue. Today he didn't relish getting thrown around.

The DI on the task force had briefed an armed entry team and on this new information a decision had been taken to breach the premises. Nash was concerned that

Donovan may be in there and she couldn't afford to have a whole team committed to a long wait when the phone work indicated where Donovan was.

They arrived in good time just as the DI finished a final welfare check and briefed the rest of his team from a car park some way from the target address. Once they all knew the address would be hit within five minutes' time, they split. Confident of their roles and responsibilities they set off to an RVP and awaited the armed team.

Nash and Moretti remained in their car as they had done on the previous occasions and waited for the radio to come to life with a positive on the arrest of Donovan.

'This is it, Nick, I reckon we've got him now. He's got nowhere to run and my money's on him knowing we had the address covered and he's waiting on us going in to die in a blaze of glory,' she said.

'Suicide by cop?' Moretti questioned.

'Yep.'

'And you're prepared to let this run knowing that?' he asked.

'I don't know it for certain, do I,' Nash stated more than she posed a question.

'Prison system's full to capacity, so one less for Christmas dinner won't hurt,' she remarked.

'Sometimes I really don't know you,' Moretti responded.

The radio breached their world.

They'd both observed the Specialist Firearms Unit stealth approach to the main door to the house. The decision had been taken to have a team enter via a ground-floor window while other armed officers entered around the back. Two slim-looking cops dressed all in black were in position at the front. A hand count was given, and on three, a pane of glass in the flat's window was smashed and a flash bang grenade thrown in to distract the suspect. What they got in return was not the surprise they'd envisaged. A backdraft from an explosion showered the lead officer with broken glass and splintered wood, throwing him off his feet into the bins in the front garden. His cover officer, in shock from the blast, sought his colleague's location.

Everyone close by heard the explosion, then time stood still for a moment. That's how it appeared to Nash and Moretti. It wasn't like an explosion on TV – nothing like it. As they watched, bits of card that had blown through the window floated down from above like Chinese lanterns, some still ablaze, others flashed red with embers. The tactical advisor instructed other armed officers to cover the lead team as additional people got the two who'd been blown backwards away to an awaiting ambulance at the RVP.

They both looked stunned and unsteady on their feet. It was no wonder. Sirens could be heard. Nash recognised them as those of the London Fire Brigade. Curtains that had covered the window were ablaze and there was a distinctive smell of gas. Both Nash and Moretti got out of the vehicle and began to assist other officers as they evacuated the houses either side. Moretti could see a cop with an extinguisher as he tackled the blaze and gained control. The tactical advisor instructed four others to enter and clear the building, satisfied the blaze had been contained and the flash bang had caused the gas to ignite. Nash and Moretti stayed outside behind a hastily erected crime scene tape and awaited further direction.

'We're in. No sign of suspect. There's a charred phone on the floor and too many playing cards to count. The gas is shut off. I don't know where it was coming from, but it was deliberate,' the lead officer said over the open radio.

The radio then went dead. Nash slumped back against a low wall. She acknowledged the transmission then turned to Moretti.

'All that running around and getting the intrusive authority for nothing, nothing!' She slammed the side of her fist against the brickwork and they went back to the car and sat back in. Her anger had got the better of her.

'Two injured officers, carnage, charred playing cards everywhere, and another crime scene at this sick bastard's behest. You'd better get on the blower and get some bodies down here to help manage it,' Nash directed. Not that Moretti needed any direction. She was beginning to feel she wasn't worthy of the rank she held when a criminal could play her like a fiddle, picking her up and putting her down for his own enjoyment. She envisioned Crockett and Tubbs back at the office with I-told-you-so grins all over their wizened faces. Nash got on the phone and made herself busy.

Moretti's phone rang out and he stared at the screen at the withheld number.

'Can you get it?' he asked Nash who pointed at her own phone that she was on.

Moretti went through the set-up of the recorder and answered.

'Finished playing games now?' Moretti said.

There was no answer on the other end, just a steady breathing and the sound of the wind.

'Such a sore loser, Moretti,' the voice replied.

'I haven't lost. Have you not had your fun now? What is it you want from me, Mark? To guess your new phone number now your other's melted?'

A silence languished at the other end of the phone. Moretti waited as the silence taunted him.

'You don't get it do you, Moretti?' the voice broke the standoff.

'Get what?'

'How damaging it was for me to be removed from my parents by you? They made a pact when they had me. That pact was to care for me and love me. You destroyed that, Moretti – you alone. They were doing the best they could with what little support they had until you came along with your big boots and state-issued badge of the almighty, and lifted me away from the only two people in the world who truly, truly, loved me.' The distorted voice invaded Moretti's skull.

'Look, I can't imagine how you must feel, how could I? We could talk about this face-to-face. I could explain so much about that day, why I had to attend to you, Mark. Fill in gaps that your memory has missed. What say we meet?' Moretti tried a different tactic, as he didn't want Mark to hang up on him.

'Talk is cheap, Nick, or is it Nicholas? Is that how your parents hoped you'd leave all the girls, eh, Moretti? Like the beauty on your boat?' The last sentence trailed like a hanging fuchsia but without the same heady scent.

'You've gone very quiet for someone who wants to talk, Moretti?' Mark's voice now undistorted.

'So, you've figured out who I am, now. It took you long enough to establish that despite all the clues I could muster. I expected better from you, Moretti, the top detective. So well thought of and respected at work, as you are. I thought I'd share something with you now, Nick,' Donovan said, his voice sounding joyous.

Moretti glanced at his phone. His battery didn't look healthy. He hoped it would hold out awhile longer. Donovan continued.

'I've been watching your boat while you've been on a fool's errand. No need to thank me though; just call it my contribution to Neighbourhood Watch. Well, *your* neighbourhood as mine's so transient at the moment.' He laughed, breaking his monosyllabic tone.

'I've learnt so much about you over the past six months, especially your penchant for a waif and stray. Pity you didn't take me on, Nick, when you lifted me from my playpen. A pen I was spending many a happy day in…'

Moretti heard the sound of breathing. Nash noticed his face had lost all colour and animation. His eyes watered.

'It wasn't like that, Mark. That playpen wasn't fit for an animal. You were surrounded by your own shit and piss.

Your naked body had given up, Mark. You were alone in there. You were only three years old, Mark. It wasn't your fault...' Moretti attempted reassurance as he fought back the emotions that had surfaced as he remembered that day. Moretti stopped and breathed. He wouldn't find a way for this sick, deluded person to see he wasn't to blame for the way he'd turned out. He could find redemption with the right help and support, even if that was within the prison system.

Donovan didn't see it that way.

'I know it wasn't my fault, you fucking pig, so don't go all *Good Will Hunting* on me!' Mark barked down the phone and caused Moretti and Nash to wince and withdraw from the handset that sat in the central drinks section.

Moretti had the phone on speaker and was recording everything. Charlotte had explained the killer wanted an audience as long as Moretti was in the crowd. Well, he was truly in the mix now and uncertain of how to play it. Neither of them had any idea where Donovan could be in relation to Moretti's home or even if he was anywhere near there. How he knew where Moretti lived was a question Moretti put down to the tracker on his car, and Donovan's legwork. He didn't have the mental space to give it much more thought. Donovan's voice broke Moretti's reflections.

'Let's not dwell on the past. I'm a man who finds enjoyment in the moment, Mr Moretti, as I'm enjoying a moment right now,' he exclaimed as he breathed deeply.

'Where are you?' Moretti asked, sick of hearing him breathe.

'Enjoying the view of a certain blonde houseguest of yours as she waves a brush across a canvas. It's soon to be covered in a blood red sky – blood supplied by your ship's slut, Moretti. Have you imagined such a scene when you've entertained her? I doubt it. Not as much as I have, Moretti. If you thought the pig's head was gauche, you ain't seen nothing yet.'

His laughter subsided with the realisation that Moretti wasn't going to react. His demeanour changed.

'I don't think this one can be saved, Nick. Your arms can't lift her out of the playpen you've created for her, you sick fuck. But I can release her from the torments of this world: the lies, deceit, oaths people make and break so easily. Why is that Nick? Why do people claim to commit to a set of values yet break them all the time? See, I'm the saviour they've been looking for. I'm the one who can extricate them from their burden of pain and guilt at not living a life in accordance with their values and principles. Values and principles taught by their gods and instilled in them from a young age by their parents. Parents I didn't have to guide me, Nick. So, just like you released me from mine and left me... left me without love to make my way in this cruel world, under the care and guidance of a pair of churchgoing do-gooders who insisted, Moretti, insisted I be grateful to the Lord for the gift of them both to care for me...' He paused and resorted to his steady breathing.

Moretti remained silent.

He was very mindful that anything he said now could tip Donovan further over the edge. A precipice he was willing to move beyond if pressed.

Donovan shattered the silence. 'It was fun while it lasted, Moretti, but like all things in life they must come to an end. I enjoyed our time together, a time for me to see you run around like a headless chicken with that slut pig of yours, just as I was when I first got placed with strangers. You see, Nick, I wasn't three forever and as I got older, the pain just got worse and worse and I couldn't see a way out,' he said as his voice began to break.

Moretti remained silent and let Donovan have the floor.

'I played the game they wanted, my carers, that is. Church on Sunday, a game of cards each night as that was an activity that promoted eye contact. Contact designed to make us bond, Nick, bond like a child and its natural mother and father. Except it didn't work. I knew I was different. I worked that out when I dropped my father's beloved handcrafted obsidian bowl and it shattered, shattered like my legs when he kicked the shit out of me for it and caused multiple fractures. The healing stone. That's what obsidian is. Did you know that, Moretti? No, I bet you hadn't worked that out. Well, I cured a couple of sinners with it, Moretti, so maybe the myth is true,' he continued.

'I was never going to let them in as I knew when I was eighteen I'd be off to find my true parents and that was when I intended to find out where you worked and deliver a photo of us all back together. Together. Defiant. United again against a system propped up by the likes of you, Moretti, and your tiny-minded band of cops,' Donovan said as he spat the words out.

Moretti could hear wind and the sound of Donovan regulating his breathing. He decided to take a chance.

'You certainly got my attention, Mark. How come you didn't find out where I worked and just get in touch? Talk things through? Why murder innocent people?' Moretti stopped, afraid to push too far.

There was a silence and Nash struggled to maintain quiet breathing throughout the call, then Donovan's voice invaded the car.

'I've been with you, Moretti. But like all things in your world you sometimes just don't want to see what's been staring you in the face. Why is that? Too painful a memory for you or was I just another unwanted drain on the state, Moretti? A child that no longer warranted space in your memory?'

Donovan continued, not giving Moretti time to reply, 'Now you see, Moretti, despite me seeing you each day, you ignored me, so there was only one way I knew I'd get your attention and have some fun while getting it.'

'How would I know you? You were three years of age when I last saw you, Mark!'

'There you have it, Nick. You couldn't even recognise a name that was right in front of you all this time. Now, back to the present; I'm bored with our talk. You have one last chance at redemption. Come and remove her from where she is and let's see who survives, eh? Will it be you or her, Moretti? You have an hour to decide whether you will sacrifice yourself. Your life in protection of the public's, keeping the Queen's peace, or the beauty on the boat dies and you will be reminded, forever, that you could've made a difference. All in accordance with your values and beliefs. Me? I'll be gone. Questions left unanswered forever to torment you, as you don't have the skill to find me without my help. I'm the host who holds all the cards, Moretti, and the house always wins… always wins…'

The line went dead.

CHAPTER THIRTY-SIX

A tap on the window alerted Moretti. Jonesy's face stared in through the driver's side window.

'Fuck me, Nick, you seen a ghost?' he said as Moretti let the window remotely slide down so he could speak with him.

Nash looked at Moretti and he appeared like he'd been in a trance that he was now fully out of. She leaned across and spoke.

'Jonesy, you're now my representative at this scene, Nick and I are needed elsewhere,' Nash said as she nodded at Jonesy and the window went back up.

They left Jonesy confused at the urgency of their departure but aware of what was expected of him. Nash activated the blue light in the front grill as she reversed.

The last thing they saw via the rear-view mirror was Jonesy stood in the road, scene tape stretched across the street behind him.

'Get on to Adam on the Intel desk. Tell him to contact me with properties that are owned or managed by the letting agency near where you live. In addition, I want them to pull up a list of high-rise buildings within fifteen hundred yards of the marina,' Nash stated as she weaved the car through the traffic towards the city.

Moretti did as directed as she drove.

'The other sites Donovan had used prior to the kill were way closer to the scene to facilitate his departure but I can't take the chance he's the same distance away this time. My gut tells me if he wants you dead then he'll also want to get away fast. He can't do that if he's too close to you; he'll need distance for observation before he's satisfied he can get to you and away. Finally, get the contact desk to get hold of the SFO tactical advisor for me to speak to. Please let this be the last time.'

Moretti listened but was unable to write anything down due to the car being thrown left and right.

'You're not going on the boat, Nick,' Nash yelled over the sound of two tones and car horn that Nash insisted on using as she reinforced her need for space on the road.

Moretti blanked the question. All he knew was that Tabatha didn't deserve to die at the hands of a maniac with a grudge. A maniac Moretti had unwittingly brought to the good folks that inhabited the marina: his sanctuary, a life that until now had been uncomplicated and entirely separate from his work.

Moretti wasn't Mark and hadn't lived Mark's life. Despite the kill-fest Mark had embarked on, Moretti was aware Mark wasn't without history. Not that he excused Mark's actions, far from it.

All he wanted, as did Nash, was Mark banged up for life or dead. Either option worked for them. Moretti's voice broke above the two tones from the car.

'I'm getting messages back from the Tac Advisor. They're available to speak now and the DI from the HTF has part of his team on the hurry up to the marina. He's assured me it will be a silent approach and a sweep of the immediate area,' he explained.

Nash got Moretti to punch a number into his phone as it was connected to the car's Bluetooth. He did and pressed the green button. After a few rings, the Tac Advisor was on the line.

'You're a busy person, Pip. What do we have this time?' Inspector Ward said as Nash explained what she knew so far.

'He could be anywhere right now, that's for certain. You might want to get a negotiator on-board,' Ward said.

'I'll have to brief another crew as mine are two down. We'll link up with another team from the Specialist Firearms Office and make our way to the vicinity,' Ward said.

'That's all I can ask right now. As soon as I know more, I will be in touch,' Nash replied conscious of a pause on the line.

'Nick, you're not to go on your boat. You do realise that, don't you? I have one target at the moment, and I don't need another in the mix. Let me deal with the suspect. Just keep him talking when he next makes contact.' Inspector Ward finished the call. Moretti hadn't replied to her request.

He concentrated on the phone as Nash drove. Nash looked at the digital clock readout on the dashboard. She'd used up thirty minutes already, but she estimated she was fifteen minutes out from the marina. Moretti spoke into the hands-free call assist, his battery nearly dead.

'Call home,' he said into the car's microphone.

'What are you doing, Nick?' Nash shouted.

'I need to warn Tabatha. She can't be left there to be killed!' he shouted back as the phone began ringing.

'Nick. If she leaves that boat, then he'll kill her. He'll know you've put a call in because he's watching her. Her body language will change, and she'll panic. He'll know you've called her and then you may as well have killed her yourself. He's expecting you to do just that, Nick. Then he can blame you again. Right now, we have a chance to find him before he–' Nash's phone began ringing as Moretti cut his own one off.

'Yes,' she said.

'It's Adam. I've looked again at the imaged hard drive from Peterson's computer. There's nothing coming up for rent *but* Peterson does have a flat that fits. I think he must have used it for himself as his call data shows pizza deliveries from a local firm.'

She prayed the signal wouldn't be lost. Due to the buildings in London there were many areas a signal could drop. Adam came back on.

'I contacted a mate of mine on the HTF and he went into the pizza place and spoke to the owners. They confirmed they'd delivered to the flat yesterday. The delivery driver wasn't on duty to speak to. The manager said they delivered two pizzas.' There was a break in the signal, then it went dead.

Nash concentrated hard on the road ahead as she threw the car in and out of traffic. Her Bluetooth earbud itched her ear but she ignored it.

'He's got Peterson at a flat near here,' she said to Moretti.

'What? What makes you say that?' Moretti shouted back.

'That last call I took. Phone data from Peterson's phone and a follow up in person showed two pizzas delivered to a flat yesterday that Peterson owns. Unless our killer is very hungry then our missing letting agent may have been found by the wrong man,' she explained.

'Great work,' Moretti responded.

'I think we've housed him,' Nash said as Moretti redialled the number for the Tac Advisor and began to explain the message from Adam and the potential address.

Inspector Ward thanked him and said she'd liaise with the HTF Detective Inspector. Nash kept her momentum on the drive. They were two minutes by car from the marina when she slowed down, parked up in a side street and terminated the engine.

CHAPTER THIRTY-SEVEN

Nash took her secure laptop from her kitbag on the back seat and brought up a Google Maps satellite view of the block of flats. As she viewed the screen, she could see the distance between the block and the marina was within range for Donovan to hide then get to Moretti's boat unseen. Moretti's boat was caught in the image.

'This is good, Nick. Donovan won't have a clue that we have the delivery information and that it's from Peterson's phone. He'll just think we've done with Peterson. I know we shouldn't work on assumption, especially with Donovan, but I'm hopeful Peterson is alive. Either that or Donovan has his phone and killed Peterson knowing he was talking to us,' Nash said as she cushioned her head on the headrest.

She was relieved Moretti hadn't been so gung-ho to get back on his boat. He'd tried his home number again, but it just rang out. Moretti's mobile phone rang.

'Moretti,' he answered, with a sense of urgency in his voice as the battery indicator blinked.

'You're a brave man, Mr Moretti, or a callous one. I can't quite make you out. I told you what the deadline was and still you've failed to appear. A phrase you lot in the filth like to use, I believe,' Donovan said.

'Mark, please stop what you're about to do. I will do anything you want but please don't go killing that girl. She's nothing to you, or me. She's a neighbour, Mark, whose houseboat's heating has failed. Mark, it's Christmas, a time when we should be finding peace with one another.'

'Peace? Peace, you say? Moretti, you have no idea what it's like to live without peace. I've spent my entire life without peace but now I'm finding it. Every life I take it brings me a sense of calm and closure. It's my duty to rid this world of those that don't keep to their word. People like you, Moretti.'

'Mark, I don't know what promises I've said that I've broken. You were so young. What promise have I broken?' Moretti pleaded for an answer and in doing so kept Donovan talking as the firearms inspector had requested.

'You remember when you were on TV, Nick? That series you did for the BBC. Running about London protecting children like a superhero?'

Moretti had been in a TV series. It focussed on a London child protection team's work.

'Yes, you're right. I was in a documentary, but I can't for the life of me think of what I said that broke any vow or promise that I made to you,' Moretti replied. 'Mark, explain to me what it is before you do anything else, please?'

Despite the coolness of the day Moretti felt hot. Nash remained silent. This was one for Moretti to handle and she didn't want to risk adding her voice into the mix and upset Mark any more than he was.

'You, Nick, made a promise to protect those children in London. To remove those at risk from harm and place them in a stable and loving home. You failed me, Nick. I was already in a loving home and you robbed me of my parents' love. You robbed me of life. The only two people in the world that loved me for who I am. Now I will rob you of a life you value; unfortunately it can't be your own as you're too gutless to face the music, Nick.'

'Mark, I had no choice. But you do. I had no choice because your father and mother couldn't care for you in the way you deserved. They were chronic drug users, Mark. They were out of it when I got to you. Your mum pulled a knife on me, for fuck's sake. I had no choice. I couldn't leave you, I couldn't leave you there. I would have neglected the three-year-old boy who looked up at me and smiled for the first time since I got into the house. The scars of seeing you in that playpen, how your smile reduced to a frozen watchfulness as quickly as it came, will remain with me forever, Mark. Please, for the love of all that's decent about you, stop, now. Just come out from wherever you are and meet me at my boat.' Moretti finished what he felt was his final plea.

'I know all that, Moretti. I saw the police file for my case along with the scene photos and an image of a knife alongside a ruler. The knife you removed from my mother, a knife similar to the one I'm holding now.'

Moretti grabbed the phone from the holder and before Nash could stop him, he was out the car, running towards the marina.

'I'm headed to the boat, Mark. Don't do anything until you see me. Don't kill her,' Moretti begged as he ran towards the gates. He fumbled for his access card in his wallet.

Nash raced out behind him, her phone at her ear.

'Moretti's bailed out the car and is running towards his boat! For fuck's sake do something now!' Nash screamed down her phone at the firearms team leader as she picked up her pace desperate to catch Moretti.

Moretti made the gate and was through, leaving it to self-shut. Nash wasn't so lucky, and the gate closed as she reached it. She began to scale the mesh as she hauled herself over the top and dropped to the other side like a Royal Marine Commando. Her phone dropped to the ground in the process as she ran after Moretti who was now approaching his boat. Nash could see Tabatha through the boat's living room window. She was wearing Moretti's Bose noise-cancelling headphones and appeared in her own world as she rocked her head and mouthed the words to a song. Moretti ran towards his front door, and bounded onto the boat and through the open door. Nash was too far behind him. As she increased her pace, she slipped and fell. She was alone in the middle of the road as she looked around.

Moretti had reached his living room and grabbed Tabatha who screamed as she hadn't heard him come in. He removed the headphones that encased her ears.

'I've no time to explain but we've got to leave,' he said as he grabbed her arm and led her out of the living room.

The headphones pulled from the amplifier's socket and the connection went back to Moretti's main music system. Idles' *1049 Gotho* blared out of the tall floor standing speakers and Moretti felt like he was caught in a film. They got outside and a voice came back on the line Moretti had left open.

'About time, Nick. Any last words before you die in front of the person you value so much in life?' Donovan said, a finality in his voice that was cold and reassured.

Moretti held the phone close to his mouth as he spoke. 'You're too late, I've got her, so go ahead and do your worse because I'm done with you,' he said exasperated.

As Mark began to laugh, the sound from the phone increased in volume as it mixed with the song from the boat.

'You're such a fool, Moretti. It was never about the girl on the boat. She was the bait I needed to lure you out. It's the other woman in your life that I'm interested in, the one you spend every day with. The one I have by the neck now, stood in the road, tears in her eyes from what I can tell through her snivelling. The throat. A part that resonates sound and worthless words… worthless words, Moretti.'

Moretti let go of Tabatha as he darted from his boat and back into the road. There was Nash. Tears in her eyes as Donovan stood as he'd said. A steel blade rest upon her throat. His face obscured by a mask of a wolf. The fur was long; it had black teeth that protruded from a realistic-looking snout. Teeth carved from obsidian. This was no off-the-shelf Halloween job. It was custom-made. Moretti looked at Nash's eyes. They watered and he thought it was the wind from her run that had caused the reaction as she was out of breath, but then he saw her mouth quiver and realised it wasn't.

Moretti put his hands up towards Donovan, palms flat, phone cradled between thumb and index finger.

'Mark, what are you doing? Get away from here! Just let her go and we can get this all sorted,' Moretti pleaded as he stepped closer to where they were stood.

A wind had picked up and dust was kicked up from the roadway and gently swirled around their feet. Nash remained calm while she felt Donovan's breath at the nape of her neck through the mouth of the mask as he leaned down and his tongue protruded out the side and slowly licked her cheek.

Nash considered what she could do, remembering Donovan was a trained fighter and knew close-quarter combat techniques well. Any move she'd try on that she'd used in her own training could be projected by her movement and read by him as an act of hostility before she'd completed it. She waited.

Moretti and Donovan stood as though they were in a Western standoff. Donovan shifted his feet behind Nash and began to move the blade gently against her throat.

'Do you know what my carer father's favourite film was, Moretti? The one he insisted I watch over and over again?' He never gave Moretti the chance to respond.

'*Restless Natives*. It was a film about two young disgruntled Scots who robbed tourists in the Highlands. One wore the mask of a clown, the other a wolf,' he said as he turned the knife edge closer to Nash's neck.

'They get captured in the end. The penultimate scene is a detective inspector like your boss here, Moretti, who opens the doors to the van he holds them in, and they all look out at the cliff edge. Do you know what he says to them, Moretti?'

Moretti swallowed. 'No. No, I don't,' he said as he kept his eyes on Nash's.

'I cannae let you go.' Donovan let out a raucous laugh as he said the line.

'I cannae let you go. But he does, Moretti. Alas, Moretti, I'm no detective inspector, you see, I'm the wolf that has no option but to take its prey to gain my freedom.' Donovan kept the knife at Nash's throat as he looked up and laughed.

Nash sensed Donovan's body tense against her. She realised if she didn't try something while she still had the breath in her body to do so, then she'd die at the hands of a madman who wore the mask of a wolf. She breathed in, shut her eyes and with as much force as she could generate smashed her heel down Donovan's shin and twisted into his body.

She winced as she felt the blade cut her neck. Donovan roared in pain and raised the knife back. She looked at Moretti as Moretti screamed, 'no!'

A clear, loud, crack resounded around them and penetrated the air.

CHAPTER THIRTY-EIGHT

The crack was followed a split second later by the sound of shouting. Nash dropped to the ground along with Donovan. Moretti sprinted towards them and bent down where Nash lay. He stroked her hair while he said her name. 'Pip, Pip, for fuck's sake say something,' he said as he visually examined her outer clothing and the blood seeping beneath them both.

Armed officers were now with them and Moretti felt a hand on his shoulder pulling him up.

Moretti stood transfixed as the macabre scene unfolded. One officer moved forward, gun trained on the heap of clothed flesh that was Donovan. Blood spread from the chest across what was once a white flannel shirt.

He checked the body and lowered the gun. The other officers who'd provided cover moved aside as paramedics were called forward now it was safe to properly assess the body. It was over. Moretti heard a sound behind him, and Tabatha appeared by his side. She wore the winter coat he saved for when he cleaned the outside of the boat.

'I thought it was you. Thank God you're safe,' Tabatha said as she joined Moretti while Nash was assisted by a paramedic to where they stood. 'I'll leave you alone,' Tabatha said before she turned and scuttled back onto the boat and into the warmth it provided.

Moretti turned to Nash. He noticed she had a dressing taped to her neck and despite her padded coat her shoulders had relaxed from the tense position they were in as she'd stood and waited for Donovan to present an opportunity to be shot. He put his arm on her shoulders and drew her close. She sank into his side and Moretti felt her relax as she released a long sigh. Both comforted in the fact they were alive. Inspector Ward approached the chain-link fence that separated the marina from the block and Moretti faced her.

'It's over, Pip. Suspect's dead. He had a hostage in the flat who's now in the ambulance being checked over. He's given his name as Neil Peterson. It's over to you now, if you're up to it, that is? I'd appreciate your control of the scene, as this will be handed over to the Independent Office for Police Conduct now. To be fair the flat's pretty empty. He was ready to kill. It was a clean shot and correctly taken,' Inspector Ward added.

Nash nodded and asked to borrow her phone, Moretti's phone's battery was now dead.

'JJ, get your arse over to Moretti's boat with a few of the team. We've got him,' she ordered.

JJ asked no more, and Nash terminated the call and handed the phone back to Ward. Both Moretti and Nash walked back towards the marina's gate where she retrieved her phone from the floor.

Moretti popped the boot to his car and took out the scene bag, checking he had at least two forensic suits left, which he did.

* * *

The pub heaved with Nash's team who, despite it being Christmas Eve, had all agreed a drink was in order before some could go home to their families. Nash didn't have the luxury of giving the whole team Christmas Day off. The investigations were far from over. The Independent Office for Police Conduct wanted access to different aspects of the investigation, as she'd expected.

There'd been no positive ID of the body at the scene. Donovan had taken a headshot and the mask had been left on. No ID was found on the body or in the flat. DNA had been taken due to the mess and they awaited results. Neil Peterson was in a state of shock at the hospital where they refused to let any officer have access to him. He'd gone into a catatonic state and needed treatment as a priority over any need of the police.

Nash shrugged it off. Peterson could wait. Where Donovan had acquired the obsidian knife would remain unknown. Association charts revealed he had the knowledge and contacts within the criminal world to obtain it. Donovan's social worker, from when he was a child, had been located, as well as the other worker he had been assigned when turning eighteen. It turned out Donovan had fallen off the radar on reaching adulthood. He was one of many and they'd done their best to try to contact him, but in the end, they'd exhausted all options.

His childhood worker described a quiet and withdrawn boy. He'd had an obsession with knives, and collected many where he could, always for display indoors. It wasn't a total surprise but nevertheless a sad and distressing thing to hear. Donovan had taken to reading the Bible at about age twelve but refused to label himself with any particular religious order as he preferred to explore them all in his own way.

His social services file made for a very sad read. A file Moretti had decided to look at while Nash sat opposite him, head back and eyes shut. They'd left the pub, as had many, keen to get away for whatever time they had left to be with their family. Both were now back in the main office at Moretti's desk. Moretti felt some sadness at the outcome. He'd wanted an opportunity to speak face-to-face with Mark, tell him whatever he wanted to know about the day he'd removed him. When Mark hit thirteen, he'd drifted into a gang and, due to his quiet nature and not being known to police, he'd been exploited and used to store drugs, guns, and any other item the elders decided.

Knives were a particular favourite. This led to Mark moving them on and he became adept at selling them and buying others. How he'd become so forensically aware Moretti put down to TV and the gang culture he'd ingratiated himself with. Nash wasn't entirely convinced but kept her thoughts quiet as there was no need to raise her objections.

'Hey?' Moretti piped up as he shut the copy of Mark's social services file. He'd been given a copy because he was still respected within the child protection side and they trusted his word as to its use and the protection of Mark's story, his childhood.

'What now? Can't a woman get some sleep before she has to contemplate another Christmas alone?' Nash muttered, looking forlornly at Moretti.

'I was only going to offer you a drink and the chance to spend Christmas Day with me here? I'll get some mince pies in,' Moretti said, hoping she'd agree. His holiday now looked as though it would happen in four days' time.

'Just get the drink and pour,' came her response as she sat up and rubbed her eyes.

Moretti smiled, took the file from the desk and opened the bottom drawer to his pod, where he kept a bottle of Scotch.

As he opened the drawer his gaze became transfixed. He slowly put the file back on his desk. He moved his swivel chair away from the pod. His eyes remained focussed below desk level.

'Nick? You OK?' Nash asked.

Moretti bent down and removed a set of Beats headphones and a lanyard with an ID attached. Nash stopped.

'Aren't those headphones the cleaner's? What are they doing in your drawer? Has he resigned?' Nash questioned.

Moretti placed the items on his desk. As he turned the ID card over, the image of Mark Donovan looked back at them. Below the image was his embossed name. An association Moretti had interrogated his brain to establish when they'd left the club. Moretti removed the drawer and upended the rest of the contents.

The bottle of Scotch rolled onto the desk. Nash prevented it hitting the floor with her hand. The amber fluid it contained moved like a caged wave. Numerous playing cards of the ace of spades and the joker littered Moretti's desk and as they jostled for space some cascaded onto the floor. He saw an envelope with his surname handwritten on. He looked at the envelope then at Nash. Nash bent down to her bag and produced a pair of latex forensic gloves.

'Just in case we've got it all wrong,' she said as she handed them to him. Moretti accepted them. His eyes a picture of sadness and humiliation.

'He was here all the time. He'd observed the investigation as we were. Every item that came across my desk he would have read, Pip. I should've cleared my desk each night of the actions, statements, lab reports, pictures, but I didn't. Always so focussed on the day-to-day investigation, I neglected the need for a clear desk. He had access to everything, Pip.' Moretti paused as he looked at the bedlam that had become his desk. One huge mound of playing cards on top of enquiry papers. He sat back, hands over his face, in remorse.

Nash said nothing. She knew Donovan would have read her decision logs as she left them in her pod, too. A pod she never locked.

She cursed herself that she hadn't acted on her own realisation that the suspect was too close for comfort by running Mark's name through HR to see if it came up as an employee. The cleaning firm he worked for was outsourced so she felt some comfort that this would've proved negative. Even so it should've been done.

Moretti stretched the gloves, put them on, and picked up the envelope. He produced a penknife he kept in his top drawer. He clicked the blade open and ran it along the seam of the seal. He continued around each side until he could lay the paper flat, which he did, on top of a white sheet of printer paper he'd retrieved from the paper tray behind him. He couldn't be certain what may drop from within it.

Inside the envelope was a Met Police Christmas card. The front was taped over with the picture of a joker he'd seen too many times before. Within the card he could see a crude metallic-looking object. It appeared like the type you'd see in a musical birthday card and he treated it as such. As he opened the card the sides separated, and comedy laughter sang out as he read the handwritten words:

Read 'em and weep, the dead man's hand again.

If you enjoyed this book, please let others know by leaving a quick review on Amazon. Also, if you spot anything untoward in the paperback, get in touch. We strive for the best quality and appreciate reader feedback.

editor@thebookfolks.com

ALSO IN THIS SERIES

COVER BLOWN (Book 2)

A London advertising executive is found dead in her bath.
Soon another woman is killed in similar circumstances. DI
Nash and DS Moretti are hunting a killer, but finding a
link between the victims is the only lead. What is it about
their social media accounts that makes them a target?

SHOTS FIRED (Book 3)

After going cold, a London murder case suddenly reignites when the weapon used is connected to murders in Glasgow and Belfast. DI Nash and DC Moretti investigate but come under criticism. Nash will have to go out on a limb but will Moretti defend her?

EVIDENCE POOL (Book 4)

When a powerful Russian oligarch finds his assistant's lifeless body in his London mansion's pool, he is quick to claim diplomatic immunity and scurry into the panic room. Detectives Nash and Moretti are convinced the killer is still in the luxury residence, so they place the building on lockdown. But it seems that all of the members of the household, family and staff alike, have something to hide.

All FREE with Kindle Unlimited and available in paperback from Amazon!

OTHER TITLES OF INTEREST

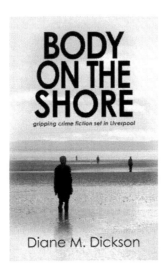

BODY ON THE SHORE by Diane Dickson

When police retrieve a body from the flat sands of a popular beach, DI Jordan Carr is presented with his first murder case. The victim is a woman, but they know little more about her. Tracing the events that led to her death will take the detective on an uncomfortable journey into the dark side of Liverpool.

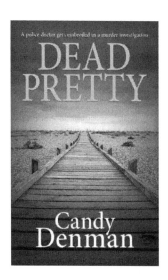

DEAD PRETTY by Candy Denman

When a woman is found dead in Hastings, Sussex, the
medical examiner feels a murder has taken place. Yet she
feels the police are not doing enough because the victim is
a prostitute. Dr Callie Hughes will conduct her own
investigation, no matter the danger.

Head to www.thebookfolks.com for more great fiction!

Made in the USA
Middletown, DE
21 December 2023